02. 04. 10

For Will —
Thanks so much
for buying my
book and showing
up for the reading.
See you at the
Onion River launch!

Cheers

Jason

THE VIDEOGRAPHER
Winner of the 31st Annual International
3-Day Novel Contest

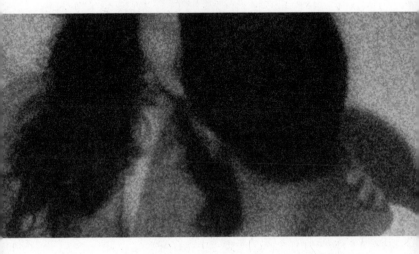

THE VIDEOGRAPHER

Jason Rapczynski

3-Day Books

Vancouver – Toronto

The Videographer
Copyright © 2009 by Jason Rapczynski

COVER AND INTERIOR DESIGN BY Mauve Page.
COVER PHOTO BY Chris Mason Stearns.
WITH THANKS TO Heather MacLean
    and Aiden Pancer.

Printed in Canada by Friesens.

Mixed Sources

Cert no. SW-COC-001271
© 1996 FSC

FSC

LIBRARY AND ARCHIVES CANADA CATALOGUING
IN PUBLICATION

Rapczynski, Jason, 1978-
    The videographer / Jason Rapczynski.

ISBN 978-1-55152-252-4

    I. Title.

PS3618.A73V54 2009   813'.6   C2009-902167-6

Distributed in Canada by Jaguar and
in the United States by Consortium through
Arsenal Pulp Press
(www.arsenalpulp.com).

PUBLISHED BY
3-Day Books
341 Water Street, Suite 200
Vancouver, B.C., V6B 1B8
Canada

www.3daynovel.com

TO MY MOTHER

WHEN I GET TO THE CLUB REGGIE'S ALREADY THERE, SITTING IN A CLAMSHELL BOOTH LIKE HE'S RIDING THE TEACUPS AT CONEY ISLAND. THIS IS WHERE WE meet and this is where Reggie gives me my assignments.

On stage, a stripper sits on a blanket, waiting for someone to approach the tip rail. Tanned and blond, she's got an airbrushed look I associate with glossy magazine covers. She's hot enough to be working a much nicer club, which explains why she looks so pissed. Plus, it's one in the afternoon and no one's here.

Reggie, he's sitting back in a blousy silk shirt, tapping the faux-leather booth pad with three of his fingers. The pinky on his right hand is missing, so that's all he's got. The shirt, it's black and gold, says Las Vegas on the back, even though you can't see it. Two enve-lopes on the table and only one of them is mine.

Music plays and looking over I see the stripper turn away from the jukebox and hop back up on stage.

With his good hand, Reggie slaps the table like a buzzer. Shouts out the name of the song like on *Name That Tune*.

He snaps the wheel of his Zippo, producing a short yellow flame. Goes, This place should have a fucking DJ.

The girls here, each one dances to the same three songs. Their official polework soundtracks. Mondays, only three girls work so it's the same nine tracks all day and night and after a while you don't even hear the music.

Reggie lights a cigarette. Snapping his Zippo closed, he goes, She looks like Marilyn.

I glance at the girl on stage and, the way she looks, he could mean Monroe or Chambers. I know he means Marilyn Chambers because Reggie refers to all his favorite porn stars this way.

This girl looks like Linda.

That girl looks like Jenna.

The girls, when they act in his movies, he refers to them as "talent."

Marilyn Chambers, Reggie says he knew her before *Green Door*. Says he knew her back when she was the cover girl on the Ivory Snow soap box. Before she was dropped by Procter & Gamble.

One time, he showed me this picture of the two of them together, back in the day.

In the picture, Reggie, he looks sort of like a young Sylvester Stallone. Says that's how come they still call him Sly. I'm not sure who he means by "they," but whoever they are, I doubt *Sly*'s got anything to do with Reggie's looks.

Black hair slicked back, he speaks with a smarmy accent, even though this is where he's from. Nowadays, he looks more like the cook in a Greek diner than the Italian Stallion.

Remember the time, he says. Remember the time you went out with that stripper 'cause she reminded you of your ex-girlfriend?

Don't start this, I say.

Remember the time.

Once, I dated a girl an entire summer because I thought her father looked like Bruce Willis. I mean, that's not exactly how it happened. This girl, I mentioned that her father looked like Bruce—she told her father—and after that he treated me like the son he never had.

Reggie, he's the father I never wanted.

He's my mentor.

My business partner.

The devil in my ear.

He doesn't own this place, but he uses it for an office.

That news report, where two girls were arrested for leaving a baby in the back of a freezing car while they got drunk at a strip club, this is where it happened. They came in for an interview and Reggie started feeding them drinks.

On the window of the car: one of those bright yellow signs that say baby on board.

When they come in to be interviewed, girls always put "bisexual" on the questionnaire.

Remember the time, Reggie says—but just then we're interrupted by police.

It's one cop, actually, and he's here for one of the envelopes.

He slides it off the table, shoots the shit and then leaves.

The girl on stage swings round the pole like a tetherball. Track marks on her arm. Music stops and she walks off like Linus with his blanket.

SATURDAY AFTERNOON AND I'M RIDING THE ESCALATOR UP TOWARD THE FOOD COURT. I LOOK TWICE AT THE GUY RIDING DOWN 'CAUSE HE'S FLOSSING HIS teeth. You gotta love the way some old people just don't give a shit. Live long enough and every second counts.

2

I'm eating Chinese food off a Styrofoam plate when my cell phone rings. In the mall food court, every restaurant's Chinese.

The China King.

The Texas BBQ.

Café Europa.

Bourbon Street Grill.

All these restaurants, all they serve is fried rice and boneless spareribs, some sort of orange or honey chicken. Rice drops off my white plastic fork as I answer the phone.

What the fuck? Reggie says. The disk you gave me's blank.

I picture him sitting in the club, his laptop on the table in front of him. A stripper, maybe, sitting on his lap.

No it's not, I say.

It's blank, he says.

And I say, Flip the damn thing over.

The disk, I mean. Not the imaginary stripper.

Ah, Reggie says. What would I do without you?

The disk he's talking about, it's what I traded for my envelope. Weekend footage from the nanny cams I set up at this rest area on I-95. Three different cameras, three different angles. If I get caught doing this, chances are I go to prison.

Did you edit yet? Reggie asks.

Yes, yes, I say.

Of course.

These spy cams, he wants them in the men's room. Above the entrance. Over the stalls. By *edit* he means cut the dead time. Leave the people in.

I'm not a *ghost hunter*, Reggie tells me. He doesn't want to spend ten hours looking at a mirror.

Last time I had ninety minutes of wet paper towels decomposing in a sink.

Last time he spent half an hour watching vermin scurry across the floor.

A broken shoelace.

An overflowing toilet.

My job performance is nowhere near good enough to be pulling this crap. Reggie thinks of me as his hired geek, his tech support.

The truth is that I'm learning as I go.

IF REGGIE CATCHES PEOPLE FUCKING IN A 3 **REST STOP BATHROOM, HE PROMISES TO BLUR THEIR FACES BEFORE POSTING THE CLIP ONLINE. AFTER** all, he says, one has to have some ethics in this business.

He sends me on trips down I-95, down to Maryland and Virginia.

Pays my gas and tolls.

Pays for my room at the Motel 6.

Reggie, he says there's a better chance of catching politicians in rest stops near D.C. Plus, it's safer not to set up in the same place twice.

Everyone drinks from the same well, Reggie says, so it's best not to keep going back.

AS I TEAR OPEN THE MANILA ENVELOPE, A 4 **TRIBE OF MALL GIRLS PASS ON THEIR WAY TO THE STAIRS. STAIRS BETWEEN ESCALATORS, LEADING UP TO THE** Showcase Cinema above the food court. The Cinema de Lux. Up there it's six dollars for a popcorn and tickets are $10.75. If you see a movie in the Director's Hall, for twelve dollars you get to choose your seat in advance.

A medium coffee, that's three dollars, which is why they won't let you bring your own. Soda, you can have it in a plastic tub for a quarter more.

Meanwhile, it's payday.

My paychecks always come in these wrinkled envelopes, every other week, wrapped in rubber bands.

Everything off the books.

Now money's spread across the table. I count out twenty $100 bills. Two grand smeared with fried grease and duck sauce.

This is twice what I normally get, but I won't ask why. I have an idea about why, but the truth is I don't want to know.

MY PHONE BEEPS, ALERTING ME TO A TEXT MESSAGE: *Never look a gift horse in the mouth.*

"Money talks": another one of Reggie's mottos.

Also: Take what you need and run.

5   WHEN I GET HOME, A MESSAGE FROM PETE ON MY VOICEMAIL. BIG NEWS, PETE SAYS, HE'S GETTING MARRIED. PETE BERMAN: MY OLDEST FRIEND. HE DOESN'T need a best man; he wants me to film his wedding.

In high school, Pete and I managed to get thrown off the school paper together. The story goes, Pete calls the field hockey coach and lies about writing an article to get this girl's phone number for me. The girl is the captain of the field hockey team, and Pete claims he needs an interview. The phone number's unlisted and the coach, she calls the school to verify Pete's story—but not before giving him the number and not before I call it.

Meanwhile, we've just submitted our first article for the paper. They sent us to review a movie, but our review turned into a story about the two of us trying to pick up girls in the theater. Nevertheless, when the principal calls us in for his lecture on ethics in journalism, he says the paper still wants to run our piece.

At our five-year reunion, the captain of the field hockey team and the coach, they show up as a couple.

Now Pete thinks I'm a videographer.

NEXT MESSAGE: YEAH, THIS IS JOE. MAKE SURE YOU BE THERE tomorrow. On time.

I'm thinking, Christ, Reggie, what have you gotten me into?

MY APARTMENT'S A TWO-BEDROOM IN A CON- 6 VERTED FACTORY IN NEW HAVEN. EXPOSED BRICK AND STAINLESS APPLIANCES, BLUE TRACK LIGHTING ABOVE the granite counter. All the amenities of a posh loft amounting to a rent I can barely afford.

Go out the back door and there's an alley where you can cut through to the Italian neighborhood. Go out the front, you're about two steps away from the ghetto.

The gray concrete building next to the alley, that's the Italian American Club, where the old Mafiosos sit on the front steps, talking.

No windows on the building, but that's how they want it.

So you can't see inside.

So you can't see what's going on in there.

A concrete fortress.

BEFORE GOING TO BED, I PLAY "BILLY JEAN" AND MOONWALK IN socks across the acid-washed concrete floor of my apartment.

It's Saturday, August 30.

Tomorrow is my birthday.

7

SUNDAY MORNING, THE THUGS ARE UP BRIGHT AND EARLY. OR MAYBE THEY HAVEN'T BEEN TO BED. THERE ARE MAYBE A DOZEN OF THEM, ALL SHIRTLESS and jacked, bodies covered in tattoos. We're all in this abandoned parking lot on East Street, a block away from the strip club. This is my one assignment for the week. I'm here to film a street fight.

Of course, technically, there's no film involved.

I've got my JVC HD camera.

My Sony UHF wireless mic.

My MacBook Pro with widescreen display.

Apple Final Cut Studio 2.0.

All this equipment, it's a basically a mobile production studio.

As I set up a tripod, a short skinhead comes over, slapping his six-pack abs.

This is Joe. Joe Six-Pack. Joe's pleased I got his message.

He points with his fingers, naming other white guys in his group:

That's Kenny.

That's Mikey.

There's Carl.

This is Wade.

Wade has a six-pack of Budweiser. Cans. Wade wants to know if I want one.

Too early for you? Joe says.

And I look at my watch.

Joe doesn't look like a Joe, but really that's none of my business. Bright red handprints on his stomach.

Reggie tell you how this works?

And for a moment I think he means the camera.

Honestly, I have no idea how Reggie hooked up with these people. Probably he knows someone who knows someone. Otherwise, he owes someone a favor.

Used to be, I'd just be filming pornography.

The objective camera.

The straight-up hardcore stuff.

Mass ejaculation started in Japan when directors found a loophole in the censorship law against showing genitalia.

In some countries, researchers find a negative correlation between pornography and aggression.

I slide my worksheet out from an envelope money came in. The first interview's about to start. Someone—Kenny or maybe

Carl—jumps from the bed of a pickup with a wooden chair. The sort of thing that gets broken across wrestlers' backs on TV. Kenny/Carl unfolds it in front of the camera. Someone else sits down.

We're rolling.

I look at my worksheet and read from the script: What's your name?

Mike D, says the guy sitting down, like he's one of the Beastie Boys.

Shaved head.

Sunglasses.

Prison tats on his chest.

Over his shoulder, I can see the other group, the nonwhites, getting ready.

Drinking.

Stretching.

Shadowboxing.

One guy, he's punching his partner's hands, no pads, no tape.

I look into the viewfinder: I see you've done some time.

I've done a little time.

Where at?

I did two and a half years at Osborn.

What'd you do?

I stabbed someone.

What for?

I stabbed this dude six times 'cause he was a rat. Gotta let 'em know, that's how I roll.

Your best fight ever?

Probably when I stabbed that guy. I expected him to stay down, but he got up and wanted to go. It was sick. Blood everywhere. Blood come shootin' out his neck.

Cut.

Mikey/Mike D gets up and stares down his opponent.

The other fighter sits in the chair.

Rolling.

Hello, I'm Manuel Cabrera.

Hello, Manuel, I say.

I'm here to fight.

Manny's bigger than the Nazi.

You've done time?

I'm here to put on a show.

Your best fight?

Check out prisonriot.com.

Cut.

I take the camera off the tripod.

Ready?

Pan around the parking lot.

Set: Tall weeds growing through cracks in the pavement. A broken chain-link fence.

Action: The fighters come out swinging. Wild lefts and rights. They're getting it on. This looks like a heavyweight versus a welterweight. The Nazi goes down.

This looks like a disaster in the making.

Mike D's left cheek flush against the pavement, Manny dives and smashes his face with a murderous right. *Crack*.

Straddling the body, Manny strikes three more times.

Crack.

Crack.

Crack.

Get in there, someone says, and I'm thinking it's over. Zoom that shit in.

Manny swinging and grunting now, lefts to the back of the head. Jumps up and lands a knee on what's left of a face.

The sounds, they turn my stomach.

They reverberate off the wall of an abandoned factory.

Filter through my UHF wireless mic.

No one, and I mean no one, deserves this kind of beating.

Another knee to the head that could break your neck.

Stop, stop, someone's saying, but it isn't me. I want to be the one who says stop but it's not in the script.

My hand shakes with the camera.

Get in there. Zoom that shit in.

Joe comes into the picture and flips his friend over.

Guttural groans and wet slurping breaths. Arms bent at the elbows, fingers pointing at the sky. Eyes staring blankly at above.

In through the nose, someone's saying. In through the nose.

Mike D, his nose is broken. His nose, it's turned upward like a pig's, but through the viewfinder, all I can see is blood. Blood runs down his face, his neck. Blood soaks through the front of his shirt.

That Treasurer of Pennsylvania, the one who committed suicide at a televised press conference, when he shot himself in the mouth with a .357 magnum so he wouldn't have to go to prison, picture that much blood.

Watch the video, you'll see what I mean.

If you haven't already seen it, you can watch it online.

Type in yahoo.com or Google it.

Type in Bud Dwyer.

Bud Dwyer video.

Type in public suicide clip.

The kids home from school that day because of the snowstorm in Pennsylvania, they saw it on TV. The live feed. The camera zooming in. The roomful of reporters shouting.

Now it's been re-aired on a public access program called *The Satanist Hour*.

Now it's anthologized in *The Traces of Death*.

Otherwise, you have to see it online.

Most of the search results, the sites that show the footage, they don't tell you why he did it.

In the video, he hands out an envelope containing his suicide note—but watching from your computer, you don't know what it says.

The camera zooming. Blood gushing from his face like a faucet.

That's one video I'm glad I didn't shoot.

Meanwhile, Mike D is breathing now, in through the nose. His breathing sounds like Jell-O being sucked through a straw. Eyes half-closed. Towel under the back of his head for a pillow.

A tap on the back of my shoulder and that means cut.

I get out my cell phone to call for an ambulance, but Wade snaps it closed and shakes his head. Hands me an ice-cold Budweiser.

Kenny and Carl carry their boy to the bed of the pickup. Wade gets shotgun with Joe behind the wheel and they peel out of there, leaving me in a cloud of white dust.

That's a wrap.

BEFORE PACKING UP MY EQUIPMENT, I GO OFF TO PUKE BEHIND MY car. Black coffee and bits of partially digested egg. It comes pouring out in painful spasms.

I'm still squatting, wiping my mouth with a rolled-up sleeve, when Manny approaches from behind. He's got his shirt on now, a beanie on his head. Towering over me.

You OK?

Yeah, I say. Fine, it's just my breakfast.

You'll get used to it, he says.

I stand and look down at swollen knuckles. Hands big as catcher's mitts. He offers me one and I take it like a bribe.

8

REGGIE'S COMPANY, IT'S CALLED REGINALD EMERLICH PRODUCTIONS. OR REPRODUCTIONS, AS REGGIE LIKES TO CALL IT. WHEN I FIRST SIGNED ON, WE PLANned to make a movie. A B-movie. A real movie with actors and a script. Reggie wanted me as his partner because I'd been to film school in New York. He wanted me to do a screenplay.

Before I worked with Reggie, once upon a time, I knew him as my neighbor. He was my next-door neighbor and for a long time I wondered about the person who lived in that house. You could see it through the woods, through the colonnade of trees that separated our yards. A white colonial.

Every weekend a different car parked at the bottom of his driveway and, after a while, I started noticing a pattern. The drivers who backed into the driveway, they all waited with their headlights off, while the ones who parked on the side of the road kept their headlights on.

Before I knew who Reggie was, I thought he was a drug dealer.

ONE DAY, THE SUMMER BEFORE I GO OFF TO COLLEGE, THERE'S a knock at the door. Two teenage girls wait outside holding pamphlets. Plaid skirts, white blouses. One has red hair and freckles; the other's a blonde.

Hello.

They're here to tell me a beautiful story about Jesus Christ. The Jesus Christ of Latter-day Saints. They're here to spread the Word.

Outside, it's eighty-five and sunny. The sun's high in the sky but it blinds me as I stand before the Mormon girls on my parents' porch.

These girls stand on front steps preaching, and you always know what they're going to say.

They sound like telemarketers.

Like insurance salesmen.

Like representatives from some police union soliciting money for slain officers over the phone.

There's a script for this, a formula.

Yes, I want to say. Tell me more. Tell me all about Joseph Smith and his golden plates.

Yes, I want to say. Come inside.

I could be anyone.

In the eighties, there was this Latter-day Saints commercial that played on television. In the commercial there's this old woman living alone, a sort of sad old woman who's supposed to remind you of your grandmother. Then you see this group of kids get together and make a pizza. They put all these different toppings on the pizza and they bring it to the old woman. They walk right up her front steps and ring her doorbell, and here she comes with this joyous look like all her children have returned home from the war.

Of course, the pizza's meant to be metaphorical. In reality, if the old woman ate the pizza with all the different toppings, she'd end up with a case of acute indigestion, which she'd probably mistake for a heart attack. But every time this commercial played, I'd want to go out and do a good deed like I'd seen on television . . .

Next thing I know, the Mormon girls are headed back down my

parents' driveway. Now I see where they're headed, and I watch from a bedroom window as they enter my neighbor's yard.

Really, I'm just curious—I just want to see—so I pull up a chair and watch as the girls ring my neighbor's bell.

I count: one-thousand-one, one-thousand-two.

The door opens, but I can't see inside. Whoever's in there is standing behind the half-open door.

One-thousand-three, one-thousand-four.

The girls enter the house, showing pamphlets like tickets to board a plane. The door closes behind them. I check my watch, sit in my chair and wait. It's getting dark.

A few days later, I see it in the newspaper, a headline about these missing girls. I look at their pictures and read the article. Bring the paper to my parents and tell them what I saw.

I have my theories:

Our neighbor's a serial killer.

A slave trader.

A psychopath.

Our neighbor has two Mormon girls tied up in his basement.

Oh, no, my mother says, you probably just didn't see them leave. And besides, it's none of our business.

My parents, for some reason, they get into a fight.

We have a responsibility, my father says, as upstanding citizens. As pillars of a community.

My mother gives him a look like *Harold, please.*

My father's name isn't Harold—but you get the idea.

So we go down to the police station. My father takes me down and talks with this female officer sitting behind bulletproof glass. From behind her window, she speaks into a microphone, all sirs and "if you will just . . ."

When the door buzzes, the cop who comes out, he's drinking coffee from a travel mug labeled DUNKIN' DONUTS. Coffee steaming from the top of his open mug, he says it's all been sorted out. The case is closed. The girls, they're no longer missing.

Powdered sugar on the collar of his starchy blue shirt, he turns and walks out of the lobby.

LATER, I SEE THE GIRLS AGAIN IN REGGIE'S VIDEOS. HIS EARLY WORK. His straight-up hardcore pornography.

The blonde, she went on to make a big name in the industry, while the redhead became a methadone addict.

Either way, Reggie says, it's better than being Mormon.

CHEWING GUM TO GET THE TASTE OF VOMIT OUT OF MY MOUTH, I GET STUCK AT EVERY RED LIGHT ON MY WAY THROUGH THE CITY. I'M ON MY WAY TO Meadows, a nursing home in my hometown. Later, I have to pick up Norman at the airport.

The home, it's located on the main road into town between an office park and a vast stretch of undeveloped land. From the outside it looks like the headquarters of a real estate scam, the sort of place you go on an all-expense paid trip where they try to sell you timeshares.

Inside, there's a lobby with tables and couches. Jack Nicholson on the cover of *AARP The Magazine*. There are TVs mounted near the ceiling, dispensers of hand sanitizer on the walls.

There's the dining room, the common room, elevators wide enough for beds.

Signs telling visitors to go sign in at the front desk.

This is ground level, the short-term residents. The ones who have the best chance of going home. The ones who, if they make it home, may not require round-the-clock care.

They're here for occupational therapy.

Speech therapy.

Physical therapy.

They're here for the ninety days of rehabilitation covered by insurance. After ninety days, if patients don't show enough improvement, they get moved to the second level.

If you get labeled "long-term" after the first thirty days, your insurance won't cover the other two months.

In the lobby, I flip to the next sheet on the clipboard. I check my watch, sign my name, and write the time.

In the space provided for the name of the person you're visiting:

_____.

I always leave that space blank.

Once upon a time, I was a volunteer in this place. Upstairs on the second level. It isn't a hard job to get. You just walk right in and ask the girl at the desk. You wait for her to get off the phone, and then you ask her.

The head nurse comes down; she wants to know if you're here for community service. A court-ordered deal. As in part of a *sentence*. What she wants to know is if you're here for discipline, or punishment.

Most judges, when they give you community service, you end up washing police cars or picking up trash on the side of the road.

But the nurses, they have to ask. They want to know why. And maybe they won't understand.

A straight single guy who went to college. Choosing to be here and not getting paid.

You could try to explain but chances are they didn't see that Latter-day Saints commercial in 1985.

Now I'm just a visitor. I come here twice a week to see the residents. The people I got to know. The long-termers on the second floor. The ones who're still around.

For two years I brought their food, changed their sheets, emptied their bedpans. It really wasn't the sort of work I'd had in mind.

But I was desensitized.

Demoralized.

Numb.

Work with Reggie long enough and you'll do anything to go back to feeling almost human.

By the end of my first year at the home, I was doing things you're supposed to be trained for: bathroom runs, sponge baths, muscle stimulation to prevent atrophy.

To prevent bedsores, you wash the patient with olive oil soap and dry by patting, not rubbing, with absorbent paper. With a cotton swab, you apply a solution of five parts antacid, one part iodine. Air-dry for half an hour. Then the medicated powder. Even when skin's topically treated, bedridden patients need to be turned every two hours. It takes two people to move a body and the nurses, they're never around.

When they're supposed to be making their rounds, they're off on cigarette breaks, sitting in the break room, drinking coffee. Talking on cell phones, mapping out their lives.

The patients they're supposed to be caring for, as far as the nurses are concerned, they already had their chance. If you're up there on the second level, unless your family makes frequent visits, chances are, you won't receive the proper care.

After a while, it got so that I was seeing sores everywhere I looked. Open sores oozing, pussing, bleeding.

Tissue damage. Infection. Cell death.

Bedsores on patients; genital sores on Reggie's actors.

Everyone an open wound.

The male actors Reggie brings in for his films, he lines them up in a fluorescent-lit hallway for inspection. Calls me in with the camera.

Number One: Lift your dick. Lift your sack. Let's see you pull back that foreskin.

Number Two: Bend over, spread your cheeks.

(Are you getting this?)

When was your last blood test? Reggie asks the guy who puts "gay-for-pay" on the questionnaire.

Reggie's actors, the men, they're also volunteers. Weekend warriors. The recurring characters of Internet porn. Most of these guys, they fuck on film for fun.

Some of them, a few, do it because they have huge cocks and maybe it's the only way they can get laid. Otherwise, they're exhibitionists who get off on camera.

Then there are the quiet types who come in nervous.

The frat boys who arrive in groups.

Hells Angels Reggie knows from back in the day.

Put an ad in the paper that says

and see who shows up.

Post an ad on Craigslist.

Post it as a flyer at your local porn shop.

At the strip club, when guys apply in person, Reggie gets kickbacks on the cover charge they have to pay to get in, when they show up with the newspaper clipping, when they show up with the flyer.

In the hallway, when Reggie spots herpes sores or a raging case of genital warts, he has me zoom in with the camera.

(Are you getting this?)

The guys who walk in with outbreaks they don't know about, Reggie splices clips from their exams into his movies.

An oozing sore. A cluster of warts.

Not a flashframe. Not a subliminal image, but a full-blown montage.

(. . .)

The camera zooming.

This is Reggie's idea of moral pornography.

New wave film art.

A commercial for Valtrex.

Sometimes, this is Reggie's idea of a joke.

He cuts his films with library shots of pigs in a slaughterhouse and animals mating in the wild.

Stills of wedding ceremonies, church confessionals, lion tamers, priests with altar boys.

The footage he shot in New York on 9/11.

The fight I just did, Reggie will find a way to use that footage, too.

Fade in: A blonde with a blindfold chained to a bedpost.

Cut to: One guy getting his face smashed in, black and white.

In the next scene: the winner of the fight, he enters the bedroom.

This is Reggie's idea of gritty realism.

Porn noir.

Cinema verité.

Sometimes, this is Reggie's idea of a plot.

Once upon a time, Reggie was my next-door neighbor.

Once upon a time, this wasn't how Reginald Emerlich made his money.

ONE DAY, REGGIE SAYS, HE'S GONNA BE FAMOUS. WORSHIPPED. Celebrated.

According to Reggie, most sex freaks, they already know who he is.

Bloggers call him Caligula.

Dr. Strangelove.

The Stanley Kubrick of Internet porn.

I've spent enough time catering to Reggie's delusions.

ELEVATOR DOORS OPEN AND I'M STANDING FACE-TO-FACE WITH THE NURSE WHO FIRED ME: NURSE BROOKS.

Evelyn Brooks.

Evelyn, the Angel of Death.

Evelyn looks like the kind of woman who'd pack Twinkies in her kids' lunches if she had any.

Twinkies and bologna sandwiches with individually wrapped slices of yellow American cheese.

Kraft singles.

Oscar Mayer.

Maybe not Twinkies, but definitely some sort of Hostess product.

But looks can be deceiving and Evelyn, she doesn't have any kids at home. She doesn't have any "rugrats," as she calls them.

This, Evelyn says, is her family. And these are her children. The patients of Meadows.

Evelyn, she lives for her work.

Why would I want to come home to *dependants*, she says, when I spend all day long taking care of them?

Live long enough and we all go back to being children.

Evelyn fired me because I started asking questions. Because I spoke with the director, went over her head.

It wasn't just the bedsores. It was everything.

Medications getting mixed up.

Allergic reactions to foods.

Patients waiting an hour for someone to come and take them to the bathroom.

Bedsores, the director tells me, are inevitable. He says no one works harder than Nurse Brooks and Evelyn, she has her own health problems to deal with.

Diabetes.

Crohn's disease.

Crippling migraine headaches.

The cane she sometimes uses, that's for a structural problem with her ankles.

Of course, the director, he didn't share everything with me. He doesn't share the real personal stuff. But the health care workers, they know what Evelyn tells them. They want to know all about her kidney stones and suspicious-looking moles.

Ask Evelyn how she's feeling today and listen to her talk.

Ask her every day for a week and you'll earn yourself a raise.

You get a personal account of her latest CT scan or MRI.

The twitching she just noticed, that's called a myoclonic jerk. This could indicate Parkinson's or multiple sclerosis.

Whatever's wrong with Evelyn, there's always a name for it.

Hypochondria comes to mind.

Munchausen's syndrome.

Munchausen's syndrome by proxy.

Evelyn's favorite patients, they're the ones who go the quickest.

They call her Nurse Ratched.

The Angel of Death.

It's all in the eyes. The first time I saw Evelyn I knew that she was crazy.

Now, standing by the elevator, she wants to search my bag. This is a routine we have. A game of search and seizure.

The bag, it belonged to one of Reggie's actors, a mailman. Says UNITED STATES POSTAL SERVICE on one side. The guy never came back for it so after a month I took it home. Every few months Reggie lets me do this, pick something from his lost and found.

The "Douchebag Inventory" is what he calls it.

Gold watches and money clips.

iPods and BlackBerrys.

The stuff that people leave behind when they take off their clothes.

Guys who come in once for the experience.

The bartender.

The taxi driver.

The delivery man in his ups browns.

Wedding rings, Reggie says. Wedding rings! Can you believe it?

People that stupid, they almost deserve to be blackmailed.

So—what? Evelyn says. Now you work for the post office? Digging around in my bag.

I laugh and hold it open.

Evelyn knows all about me. She knows what I do for a living because, once, she had me followed. A sort of background check. Around the time I met with the director.

Evelyn's got my home address, my credit report. She's got pictures of me in a motel room, taking pictures.

I don't know this for a fact. I only know what Evelyn tells me.

One time the shades were broken and Reggie, he says I'm an idiot for not covering up the windows.

Digging around in my bag, Evelyn's looking for anything she can confiscate.

Painkillers.

Alcohol.

Pornography.

If she catches me smuggling contraband for the patients, chances are, she'll have me arrested.

You can pick *this* up on your way out, she says, breaking the seal on a sixteen-ounce stainless steel thermos of Starbucks coffee.

Look, I go. It's decaf.

This, Evelyn says, is a *drug*.

I close my bag and step inside the elevator.

11 UP ON THE SECOND FLOOR I TURN MY CELL PHONE OFF AND START DOWN THE HALLWAY. I TAKE A RIGHT AND THEN A LEFT AND ENTER ROOM 211.

Inside, it's like all the other rooms on this end of the building: mounted TV, closet space, two beds with a curtain divider. Windows looking out over a vast stretch of nothing. A barren field.

Murray, his bed's closest to the window, on the other side of the curtain.

I walk around to the other side and find the bed empty. Neatly made with hospital sheets.

I turn and whip open the closet.

What'd you think I died?

Murray.

Murray with his walker.

Murray with a gigantic orderly who looks like an NFL lineman.

The orderly stares at me dumbly like he's trying to remember my name.

You wanna take him outside?

Murray framed in the doorway: What am I?—a dog?

I wish. Dog walkers get paid more than I do.

The orderly scratches himself and limps off down the hall.

Murray rolls his walker past his comatose roommate and sits down on his bed.

He's wearing a flannel bathrobe.

A hospital bracelet.

Glasses with Coke-bottle lenses.

A network of varicose veins grips his shins and ankles.

Above the V of the robe, his chest and neck appear to be coated with a layer of Vaseline.

So—did you bring it?

Sorry, I say. It was seized upon my arrival.

The witch?

And I nod. I thought she'd be on a break.

Don't sweat it, Kid.

I open the mailbag and pull out a book: a Roycroft *Hamlet* printed in 1902.

Brought you a little gift, though.

Once upon a time, Murray taught Shakespeare at the University. Back in the day, he used a pseudonym to publish mystery novels with Shakespearean plots. Books about actors being murdered on stage during famous death scenes.

Macbeth's was always his favorite. Death.

This is too much.

I turn, look out the window. Turn back.

Holding *Hamlet*, Murray's fingers work the leaves with a delicate quickness. His hands perform movements with the ease of a professional cardplayer. He caresses the pages, strokes the half-suede binding. Traces lines of the title page like he's reading Braille.

This is quite a gift, Kid.

Murray, I say, that book's barely older than you.

With his Coke-bottle glasses he looks like Burgess Meredith in an old *Twilight Zone* episode. Without his glasses, he's legally blind.

I look down at the open book. Large type, wide margins.

How's the print? I say. Can you read it?

This is quite a gift, Murray says.

12 IN THE HALLWAY, I WATCH OUR REFLECTION IN THE STEEL DOORS OF THE ELEVATOR AS WE WAIT FOR THEM TO OPEN.

Inside the elevator: a surveillance camera, a signed certificate. The walls of the car are padded. Padding frames a panel of buttons; I push one and we ride the elevator down.

On the first floor, patients sit in wheelchairs outside the dining room.

They sit around tables, staring up at televisions. Staring at nothing.

They sit around tables, playing board games, playing their cards.

This is not the place to be if you're trying not to be depressed.

Hello, Glenda, Murray says as we pass her.

Hello, Gloria.

Hello, Doris.

Mildred, she says the food here is excellent and she's having a lovely time. She wants to know what time the band goes on, and have we been to see the Captain?

Hello, Clara.

Hello, Margaret.

Margaret waves, but in the wrong direction.

Mildred, she thinks she's on a cruise ship. According to Evelyn, Mildred was on board the *Titanic*.

On the wall, I press a bright red knob like the Staples *easy* button. Doors open automatically and we walk out into the courtyard. We walk the paved path through a maze of gardens. Sit down on a concrete bench.

Got a smoke? Murray says.

You know I quit.

Come on. I know you're holding.

Murray, I say.

And he says, What?

Never mind.

I bring out a fresh pack and strip away the cellophane. Peel back the petals of foil. Tap one out.

Murray takes the cigarette, breaks off the filter. I light it for him.

TEDDY: HELLO. MURRAY, IS THIS YOUR GRANDSON?

13

Murray looks at me and then up at Teddy.

Do we look like we're related?

Hand cupped around the cigarette as he smokes. We do this every time.

Teddy, he watches from his window all day long, leaves his room whenever he spots people talking in the courtyard. Seventy-one years old, he's here after a car accident. A collision on the parkway. Lucky to be alive. Three months of rehab and his family thinks this is the best place for him.

Hello.

Teddy waves through Murray's smoke like you'd swat at a fly.

Murray—

Hi, I say. I'm Murray's grandson.

Wind picks up.

The sound of traffic from the main road into town.

With the palm of his hand, Teddy mats down hair that's grown back. White hair wild in the breeze. He wants to know what it is I do.

Out of the corner of my eye I see a streak of white. I turn and see a nurse coming at us like a 250-pound linebacker.

Hello, Nurse Sweeney.

Teddy, the nurse says. You're not supposed to be out here.

She says, You *know* you're not supposed to be out here.

Unsupervised, she says.

Have you met Murray's grandson? Teddy says. He's a . . . what did you say you do again?

The nurse rolls her eyes. An exasperated look, but she also seems curious about the answer. She's heard about me from Nurse Brooks. She knows what Evelyn's told her.

Usually, I tell Teddy what I tell most people I meet. I tell him I'm a cameraman.

A videographer.

As in weddings and Bar Mitzvahs. As in corporate training videos.

Some people, when I want to make myself sound interesting, I'll tell them half-truths.

I do odd jobs on movie sets.

I work for a director.

I'm a documentary filmmaker.

A screenwriter.

I film jackass stunts and street fights for idiots who wannabe the next YouTube sensations.

Sometimes, when people ask, I'll tell them part of the story.

MURRAY, HE KNOWS THE WHOLE STORY. OR MOST OF IT SO FAR.

Said he overheard Nurse Brooks talking about me.

Said she came into his room and asked if he knew the truth about his friend.

In this place, Murray knows more than anyone. Murray's been here longer than most patients. He came here after suffering a stroke, back when I was still a volunteer. They put him up on the second floor and all of a sudden he's walking around. Hadn't spoken a word since coming in.

Then one day I see him in the hallway, wandering, and he goes, What day is it, Sunday?

And I have to check my watch.

Yes, I say. As a matter of fact, it is.

BACK IN ROOM 211 I PUT WHAT'S LEFT IN MY BAG IN MURRAY'S CLOSET.

Notebooks and pens.

A prepaid calling card.

An iPod for classical music.

The closet's filled with extra flannel robes and Nike sweat suits.

Tempur-Pedic pillows.

Afghan blankets.

A pair of sheepskin slippers.

Murray's books are in there. A replica Maltese Falcon I bought on eBay.

I plug an air freshener into the wall.

So tell me, Murray says. Have you found a nice girl yet?

We do this every time.

Tell me, Murray says.

And I always say no but I haven't been looking.

But Murray, he wants to know when I plan to settle down. Start a family with a nice young woman.

The house.

The cars.

The keeping up with the neighbors.

Most women my age, they're already married or already divorced.

I tell Murray I just can't do normal for whatever reason. I'm just not feeling it.

And maybe what I mean is I never have felt it.

Mishigas! Murray says. A copout.

Doing a normal thing makes you feel normal, he says like George Burns playing God.

Make your bed in the morning.

Do the laundry.

Go for a walk in the park.

I could adopt a pet.

Go to the singles bars.

Register for an online dating service.

Fill out the compatibility questionnaire.

Get out of the business.

Murray, he keeps up with the world outside. He knows what's going on.

Other people here, they're living in different worlds. Worlds of rotary phones and TVs with antennas. Frozen dinners that you heat in the oven.

They're living in worlds of typewriters, radios, bad wallpaper, cigarette ads, mercury thermometers, and lead-based paint.

Once upon a time, if you wanted to see a movie, you had to watch it on the silver screen.

Before TIVO and DVDs.

Before VHS and video stores.

Before the Internet and digital cable.

Back in the day, before you watched a movie on HBO, this guy's voice would go, *The following movie has been rated ____ by the Motion Picture Association of America . . .* and the rating would show up on this blue screen and the only way you'd even know what was playing was if you knew which sofa cushion the *TV Guide* was wedged under.

Now all you've got to do is hit the information button on your gigantic remote and your TV tells you what's on and when it ends.

Hit it again and a synopsis appears at the bottom of the screen—everything you need to know about what you're watching—and all it's really telling you is the whole world's gone to hell.

16   I SPOT A COP THROUGH THE REARVIEW MIRROR SO I POCKET MY CELL PHONE AS I PASS THE STOP & SHOP ON ROUTE 63. I'LL HAVE TO WAIT TILL I GET home to call Pete back. After I call Pete back, then I'll call Reggie.

As I drive, I play half a conversation in my mind, what I imagine I'm going to say:

Reggie, I'm finished.

I've had it.

I'm done with this shit.

You need to come by and get your equipment.

Or:

Reggie, you're a predator. A scumbag. An evil corruptor . . . A skidmark on the underpants of society.

Or:

Consider this my two weeks' notice.

I must tender my resignation.

Or:

FUCK YOU, MOTHERFUCKER! DIE!

Already, I feel bad about the things I haven't said to Reggie.

17   WHEN I SAW THOSE MORMON GIRLS DOING PORN, I DIDN'T HAVE TO ASK REGGIE HOW HE CONVERTED THEM BECAUSE I ALREADY KNEW. REGGIE SEES WHAT you want most in this world, and then promises to give it to you.

Back home I decide to call Reggie first. Straight to voicemail just as there's a knock on my door. Snapping my cell phone closed, I peer through the window to see who it is.

The window in my door's shaped like a diamond and through the thick glass I can see the top of a head.

Black hair. Elvira black. Bangs.

And that's all I can make out.

I unlock the door and open it.

Whatever it is, I'm not buying it.

Hello.

Hello.

I'm Emma.

Hello, Emma.

Missy's daughter.

Missy's what?

Your daughter.

Hold it.

(. . .)

I look at this girl framed in the doorway:

Black jeans, T-shirt.

Braces and a backpack.

Ninety-five pounds, soaking wet.

What parents say, about how they'd recognize their kids anywhere, well, I'm trying not to believe it.

Um, look, there must be some mistake here. I mean, I'm not your father. I'm not anyone's father.

For sure.

Look, she says. I know this is really unfair and you must have a lot of questions right now but, please, I need your help.

Please, she says.

And I say, What?

Please.

What are you?—sixteen?

And she says, I'm *twelve*.

I do the math.

She says, I'll be thirteen in four and a half months.

It's Sunday, August 31. Today is my birthday.

---

19 IT'S THE SUMMER AFTER MY FRESHMAN YEAR AND I'M WORKING AT A SANDWICH SHOP IN MY HOMETOWN. THE PLACE, IT'S OWNED BY THIS OBESE couple, Larry and Molly, and during my first week there all the employees joke about how they fuck on the dented storage freezer in back. Larry has double chins flapping down his neck and his stomach's this enormous mass that starts below his chest and sags down halfway to his knees. Forearms covered in Jesus tattoos, he chain-smokes ultra-light cigarettes in the same voracious manner he devours a foot-long BLT loaded with mayonnaise and twelve strips of bacon. Most days, Molly stands behind the counter and complains about how long it take sandwiches to get made, as if criticizing employees in front of customers is sufficient compensation for the general sordidness of the place. It's a shit job and, before I'm there a month, half the staff has quit.

Sometime in June of 1993 I notice an application form pinned to the bulletin board in back. The applicant is Missy May. An English major from the University of Maine, she's listed just about every other fast food franchise under EMPLOYMENT HISTORY.

In each of the columns provided for contact information, she's written "Store closed."

I meet her a few days later outside the store and not long after that I overhear her telling Molly that her parents kicked her out. Then one night I invite her to Pete's house when his family's away and we sit out on the deck in a moonlit yard surrounded by suburban woods. She keeps on pouring shots . . . and the next morning she walks six miles in sandals on the hot pavement of Route 63, walks all the way to my parents' house where she shows up in a pink polo shirt and Capri pants, sweating. This time her parents really have kicked her out, so she stays with Pete till his family returns, then gets a job working at a crafts store on the Post Road.

Meanwhile, my hours at the sandwich shop have been cut. By this time, I'm the only employee who's old enough, so I'm forced to come in for a few hours each night to close the store. Then my parents start getting on my case, going on about how during their summers home from school they worked overtime, so I get two more jobs and start putting in ninety-hour weeks. During the days, I work customer service in the electronics department at Service Merchandise and spend hours hiding in the stockroom, pretending to look for VCRs and cordless phones. I still work evenings at the sandwich shop, from seven until ten, and after that I go in to work the night shift at The Christmas Tree Shops, stocking shelves and breaking down pallets. The place is located on the Post Road next to the crafts store where Missy works and, for a while, she lives in the motel across the street. When I finish my overnight shift, I drive over there at seven o'clock in the morning and spend an hour with Missy before going in to Service Merchandise.

By the middle of July, Missy's living with a married couple in a two-bedroom condo on the shoreline in Milford. The wife, she's a cashier at the crafts store and Missy lives in a spare bedroom and sleeps on a mattress on the floor. When I go to visit, the floor of the room's covered with Missy's paintings and drawings. Water colors, colored pencil. She doesn't have much else.

Then she's ten days late for her period . . . She's two weeks late. We figure she's pregnant already, so I don't pull out.

In September, I take her to have an abortion then I return to college in Vermont. After that I get back together with this girl I dated freshman year and, during the fall semester, I buy a Siamese cat at the University Mall in South Burlington. I'm living in a single dorm room and at first the R.A. doesn't seem to mind, but then some students start to complain about the howling that comes from my room and the scratching on the walls. I start getting calls from the Dean of Student Life so I give the cat to my girlfriend to keep in her townhouse.

Then one night we're in Montreal with another couple and something happens. The four of us, we're sitting at a table in this bar on St. Catherine Street and I start thinking about Missy. It's strange. Like I can sense her. Like she's right there, sitting at the table with us. I know then that she should be there and not long after that I call and she drives down from Maine for a visit. It's around the holidays, just before Christmas.

At the beginning of the next semester, the spring of my sophomore year, Missy and I take our own trip to Canada. We stay at the Queen Elizabeth Hotel on René Lévesque Boulevard in Montreal. We walk the streets, drink in bars, gamble at the casino. We tour the strip clubs and Missy looks on and laughs as I sit through a lap dance she's paid for.

Missy, she's paying for the entire trip, but I don't ask how she got the money. She says she's working at a strip club in Bangor, but only as a waitress. It's an old line, sure, but what do I know? It's easier just to believe her.

After that she visits me every other weekend, driving down from Bangor, Maine, at 3 a.m. after she gets out of work. During these visits we walk up and down Church Street in Burlington, go out to restaurants and the movies. On campus, we sit in the library, exercise in the sports center, feed the birds that flock outside the dining hall.

Then one day my girlfriend shows up at my dorm room when Missy's there. There's a big scene and I really don't know how to handle it, so I break up with my girlfriend and give my cat to Missy to take back to Maine.

Next thing I know, pictures start arriving in the mail.

Here's one of the cat in bed.

Here's one of it wrapped in a blanket.

And here, in the next one, it's leaping from a stovetop.

All summer long, pictures like ransom notes each week in my parents' mail. Junior year I move off campus with the cat, into my first apartment. It's a small one-bedroom apartment on the third floor of a firetrap building near the North End of Burlington. Missy comes down for her visits and, for a while, we're getting along.

In December, she rides a Greyhound down to Connecticut to spend the holidays with my family and I go around with the video camera filming Christmas, but after we sleep together a few times, she tells me how she was drugged and raped at this Christmas party in the strip club where she works. She tells me, the club owner, he does this to dancers to make pornography and she just wants to put it behind her, so I suggest that she move into my apartment and she drops out of college to come live with me.

In January, I drive to the University of Maine at the end of winter break so that Missy can pack up all her worldly belongings and load them into my car. The campus is dead quiet and covered in wet snow—the sound of my weighted car's tires on slush like the peeling of endless strips of Band-Aids off skin—and by the time we make it off the grounds it feels like we're on our way to everything you could ever hope for out of life.

Only my apartment's really not big enough for two people. The place is technically a one-bedroom because each of the rooms has a window, but in essence it's a converted attic space divided in half by a thin makeshift wall. In the living room, an enormous furnace keeps the place warm during the cold months that we're there, but it also emits small amounts of carbon monoxide that elicit a sporadic response from the CO detector. The smoke detector also goes off on occasion, most notably when one of the burners on the gas stovetop is involved in a small explosion that singes off Missy's eyebrows and some of her hair. But the rent's $395 a month and we're living together and, for a while, it's good.

We eat our meals together, read to each other in bed.

Watch movies.

Have sex.

Drink wine.

We go shopping together at the local supermarket and buy cuts of meat I don't know how to cook.

But after I discover some photos of Missy on stage, that's when we start fighting. We start arguing over little things, getting on each other's nerves.

One night, she's escorted home by police after running barefoot into the snow.

Another time, I go out to purchase Ben & Jerry's with our last few dollars, our laundry money, and when I return we fall into a fight and I throw the ice cream in the trash.

The next time we have money we go out to this club where I want to drink but Missy wants to dance. Two guys are sitting at the bar with us and they want to know if we're together. For some reason, I laugh and tell them Missy's my sister.

Are you joking? one guy says.

And I say, Hell no, I'm serious.

Oh, yeah, his friend says. I can see it now. You do kinda look like you're related.

You want to dance with her? I go.

And the friend says, You don't mind?

And I say, Look at her, man, the girl wants to dance.

So off they go, out on the floor, the club music playing, the lights flashing and the pounding of the bass. And this is what I wanted. I wanted to watch Missy with another guy. I knew how she was but I wanted to see for myself. I wanted to see her in action. She doesn't disappoint.

After that we break up. Missy moves back to Maine and it's about six years before I hear from her again.

AFTER GRADUATION I RETURN TO CONNEC-
TICUT TO LIVE WITH MY PARENTS AND ONE DAY
THERE'S A KNOCK ON THE DOOR. I OPEN IT AND THERE'S
Missy's father, looking disheveled and slightly insane. This guy, I've
met him only a couple of times before, the first time when I got
my car stuck after backing over a log in his driveway and he came
down off his front porch laughing. Now he says this is pretty difficult for him, but—man-to-man—he's looking for his daughter and
he wants to know if I have any idea where she is. He says he's hired
a private investigator and he knows all about the movies. He says of
course my name will have to go in the report, but if I want to coop-
erate, now's the time. I have no idea what he's talking about, except
obviously he thinks his daughter's doing porn, but the whole time
he keeps looking over my shoulder like he sees something inside
the house. He basically looks like he's about to murder me, but I
can't help feeling sorry for the guy. The truth is, I never really got
over Missy and I know how it feels when someone runs off and
there's no way of ever reaching out. Even when Missy and I lived
together, she was a mystery to me.

Deep down, I must have believed that I'd saved her from something, that I was inherently superior to her alternatives. Date rape
or a white trash family.

Or maybe that was how I needed to feel.

Empowered.

In order to justify myself.

In order to define my role in the relationship.

In any relationship, one person always has the dominant role.

There's alpha, and there's omega.

The beginning, and the end.

One way a relationship can work is when one person tricks the other into thinking he's something he's not.

But Missy was different. When I met her in college, she was unlike anyone I'd ever known. Thrift shop dresses, fake fur, Wayfarers . . . this girl was beautiful and smart and damaged. She was raised by her mother, followed her mom from state to state until finally her father got custody.

After that, she'd just run away.

The next school. The next state.

High school was Missy's tour across America.

Then she moved in with me and, for a while, it was good. But at the same time she always kept a bag packed as if she might be forced to decamp at a moment's notice.

NOT LONG AFTER THAT MY PARENTS' HOUSE IS BROKEN INTO— someone pries open the front door with a crowbar but nothing is stolen—so naturally I assume this is the work of Missy's father.

THEN ONE DAY I GET A CALL FROM MISSY. SHE'S BACK IN TOWN RECONCILING WITH HER FAM-ILY AND SHE WANTS TO STOP BY. I HAVE PLANS TO GO TO New York to visit Pete Berman that weekend and Missy, she ends up going with me. For the last year or so, I've been planning a move to New York.

We take the train to Manhattan to visit Pete, who's living near Central Park and working on Wall Street. Pete's dating a girl named Lisa. The first time I see her she's wearing the kind of little black dress thousands of girls wear each night in the city. Pete met Lisa at Harvard. He says she's the kind of nice Jewish girl his mother would've picked for him. His mother's never met Lisa, he tells me, but she approves of what she's heard. Lisa's taking a year off to work and save money before going to medical school.

On the sidewalk in front of his Upper West Side brownstone, Pete flags down a cab and the four of us head out to get drunk at the Windows on the World bar atop the North Tower of the World Trade Center. I've never been there, but on the way over, "Windows on the World" makes me think of old sci-fi films; I have an image of Earth in the distant future when the planet's encased in some transparent shield.

The way I picture it, I'm out in space somewhere, looking in.

Meanwhile, I'd prefer drinking in some trendy East Village establishment like KGB, but the girls, they have this idea about only going to the best places while they tour the city. They share the sentiment for different reasons, but I know better than to object.

Missy's brought along a disposable camera to take pictures of us getting drunk on the 107th floor of the World Trade Center . . . and later she sends me the photos.

In the first ones it's still light out and you can see the city below, small and quiet the way cities look from an airplane that's started its descent. In the later pictures, the windows are dark; black glass reflects the camera flash behind drunken poses like celebrity mug shots.

During the cab ride back, for some reason, we fall into an argument over money. The problem is, drinking up there on top of the world, I spent all mine, the cash that I brought for the trip. I realize this when I open my wallet and all I find's a classified ad I clipped out of the newspaper:

> Construction trainee
> No experience necessary
> Must have competitive edge
> Sports background A+

When I show this to Missy, she says I should call to set up an interview as soon as we get back. This bothers me . . . Why does she care if I have any money? I tell her it's none of her business whether or not I have a job. After all, it's not as if we're together. And besides, I don't want to think about seeking employment in the midst of my weekend spree. It's a buzz-kill.

Sticking my head out the cab's open window, I look up at the aisle of sky. What troubles me now—and for the rest of the trip—is this idea that our roles have somehow reversed. That somehow, I've become the one who needs saving.

But Missy, she's still the kind of girl who knows how to have fun. I mean, she looks at things a certain way. Like the most mundane details seem new and exciting to her. And this perspective rubs off on other people.

I've looked for other girls like this. Survivor types with a passion for living. Audrey Hepburn with a cat. But sooner or later they give up. They lose their basic optimism, or whatever it is that makes them see opportunity where others see none. I suppose that's what happens after you leave your family behind, after you're told what you're worth in terms of money, after abortions and failed relationships. And yet I've always found myself attracted to these girls, as if by being with them I might view the world in a different way.

Meanwhile, since graduating from college, I've been averaging a new job every few months. I can't stay in one place. I've worked for a variety of franchises and corporations. I've been employed by bookstores, video stores, furniture stores; I've worked at a movie theater, a hospital, a shopping mall kiosk. I've worked at fast food restaurants, a discount department store. I've worked weekends and holidays. Late shifts and night shifts. I've worked through forty-hour weeks and eighty-hour weeks and one wasn't any worse than the other. When you were there it was a mind-numbing grind and when you were home you dreaded going back. And when you went back no one, and I mean no one, ever failed to remind you where you were. Customers, store managers, beaten-down co-workers: they were always there to put you in your place.

Back at Pete's place, Missy says she has something to tell me, so I say, What is it? She says, Another drink first, so we have one and then we have another. We're drinking Pete's liquor, the good stuff. Pete, he's gone off into his bedroom with Lisa.

At some point, we end up going for a walk. A late-night stroll through Central Park. A place for a serious talk.

The pregnancy, Missy says. It would have been a girl.

Too early to be sure, but Missy, she just knew.

If we had it, Missy says, I would have named her Emmanuelle.

She writes the name down on a scrap of paper—a napkin she took from the bar—in case I ever forget.

Back at the apartment I drink till I black out and the next day, Missy, she won't speak to me. When I ask her why, she says, You don't remember? You don't *remember*? Well, if you don't remember I'm not going to tell you why!

After that we ride the subway to Grand Central, board the Metro and sit on hard plastic seats as the train begins to move underground. I'm sitting in the window seat. I notice the window's smashed near my head—the way bulletproof glass looks in movies when someone fires a weapon at close range. The break's on the inside, in roughly the shape of a fist, with long, thin cracks intersecting at the center. It looks like a fossilized spider, rendered in amber, with dozens of spindly legs. As the train picks up speed, it appears the legs are *moving*, rotating counterclockwise, against the fluorescent lights of the tunnel. All those legs spinning, going nowhere.

BACK IN CONNECTICUT I CALL THE NUMBER ON THE NEWSPAPER CLIPPING. I'M CURIOUS ABOUT THE JOB. I'M CURIOUS ABOUT WHAT A CONSTRUCTION trainee does. I picture myself touring a dusty job site in Carhartt overalls then drinking beers with the guys after work. After I've had the proper training, maybe I'll be one of them. Maybe this is where I'll fit in. The voice on the phone gives me directions to a corporate park. I'm going to find out.

I arrive at the office around two o'clock on a Monday afternoon. The boss steps into the waiting area and calls me in. I follow him down the hall into his office and he tells me to close the door. I sit in the small plastic chair across from his desk. He's got my résumé out on the desk in front of him. I watch as he looks it over.

I see you did well in college, he goes. Did you work hard to get those grades?

I'm a hard worker, I tell him.

And you played baseball.

He holds up the page.

The Great American Pastime.

I stare at him across the desk. He's a large man behind a large desk, but he seems out of place somehow—like Chris Farley playing a motivational speaker on *Saturday Night Live.*

The windows in the office look out onto a construction site across the street. I can see my car out there in the lot. My car is a piece of shit. All of a sudden, I hate my car for bringing me here.

Outside, it's seventy-five and sunny. Out there, construction workers hoist beams in their hardhats and cutoff sleeves, biceps bulging, like the guy in the Village People. At least, that's how I imagine them. I can't actually see them from here.

Then I notice the boss is still talking. I notice his name is Jim. The nameplate on his desk indicates this.

So . . . Jim's saying. Tell me the one quality that you need in order to be successful.

I don't know, I say. Passion?

Well, passion's a good thing to have, Jim says, but there are other things you need that are even more important. There's a formula for success, you know. And if you follow that formula you'll be successful. There's no easy way to get there and there are two kinds of people in this world—those who have ambition and those who take the path of least resistance. Do you understand what I'm getting at?

Absolutely.

Good. That's good. Because we have a structure here that's been in place for a long time and if you stick with it you stand to make a lot of money. I'm talking from experience, son. I started with this company thirty years ago. I was fired from this job five times in my first month. But I wouldn't quit. They told me I couldn't do it and each time that made me try even harder. I come from a small town, you know, my parents were poor and I was the first one in the family to go to college. Then I was in graduate school—doing my substitute teaching—and I realized something. I realized I was just a babysitter—which is fine if that's what you want to do, if you want to do the same job and make the same money year after year, but I wanted something more. I wanted the opportunity to be my own boss.

He pauses and I nod like he's just explained something I've been wondering about for many years.

Tell me something, Jim says. What are your goals? Where do you want to be in three years? Where do you see yourself in five?

I'm not sure, I tell him.

Well, that's just it. That's what I'm talking about. You know, ten years ago they did a survey at Harvard College. Only twenty percent of the students there said they wrote their goals down on paper. But do you know what happened to that twenty percent? I'll tell you: they *achieved* their goals.

What happened to the other eighty percent?

How should I know? They're probably still paying off their loans, Jim says, and laughs. Anyhow, what I'm offering here is the opportunity for advancement. What I mean is, this isn't a *job*. A job's where the employees only have control over ten percent of the company. The other ninety percent is the corporation. Here it's the other way around. Here *you* have control over ninety percent of the company. This is a *career*.

I see, I tell him. But to be honest, I still have no idea what you're talking about. I mean, what exactly is the position I'm supposed to be interviewing for?

I glance over at Jim's novelty wall clock: a picture of a leather-clad Elvis framed on its face.

Listen, he says. That's all right. This isn't like any other business. We go out and *get* our clients. We don't wait for them to come to us. But you'll learn all about that later on. This is only the first step. We have a three-step process here. I've got a dozen more people coming in today.

According to the Elvis clock, it's already two-thirty.

Understand, what I'm looking for is someone to take over this office. Someone who will eventually be sitting here behind this desk conducting his own interviews. We have three offices here in Connecticut and two more in upstate New York. Next month we're opening one in Springfield. Vinny—who runs this office now—he's going to be moving up there. So everyone here's sort of getting promoted. We're expanding, see. Three years from now I'll be setting up shop in Chicago. I've got some family out there. But the bottom line is I've got some positions to fill. A business can't grow if you don't replace the people who move up the ladder, but I'm not looking for people who want to do just enough to get by. I'm not looking for people who are concerned with how much they can make right away. What you should be thinking about is how much you could be making five years from now. My first year with the company I made fourteen thousand dollars. The next year I made forty. By my third year I was making over one hundred thousand dollars a year and that's gone up every year since.

After Jim's finished talking he tells me to show up for orientation. Thursday morning. He says I'll find out all the details then. He looks at me, head cocked, like I'm a fish on a hook—then reaches his big hand across the desk.

23

THE FOLLOWING MORNING THE PHONE WAKES ME UP JUST AFTER NINE AND I ANSWER IT. IT'S PETE BERMAN, CALLING FROM NEW YORK.

We're under attack, Pete goes. Turn on your TV.

I turn on the television; the picture fades in to a replay of United Airlines Flight 175 crashing into the World Trade Center.

I change the channel and I'm seeing the same thing.

Next channel, and you get a different angle.

North Tower, South Tower.

CNN.

MSNBC.

Video footage of people running through the streets.

Change the channel: you see the people jumping.

Change the channel: demonic faces in the smoke that billows from each tower. The smoke plume in the sky.

You see the people falling.

You see people running in the streets like in the old Japanese *Godzilla*.

And Pete says, God.

God, Pete says, Are you seeing this?

Fingers wrapped around the phone, the receiver pressed against my head, and I can hear Pete breathing on the other end of the line.

I SHOW UP FOR ORIENTATION BRIGHT AND **24** EARLY. BY EIGHT O'CLOCK THERE ARE SIX OF US, SITTING AROUND A TABLE IN A CLUTTERED ROOM. THERE'S a podium at one end of the table with a dry-erase board behind it. At the other end of the table, a blackboard displays a graph with names and dollar signs scribbled in chalk.

Jim enters the meeting room wearing a used car salesman's polyester suit.

A moment of silence.

At the podium, Jim says he's interviewed sixty people and narrowed it down to six.

Panning around, I study the other five people sitting at the table.

They look desperate, confused. They've got notebooks and legal pads fanned out in front of them, complimentary coffee and donuts.

No windows in the room, but there's a door with an exit sign that reads EMERGENCY ONLY.

I'm seriously considering it.

Half an hour later, Jim's still talking. I tuned out after the part about how he'd made varsity as a freshman on the offensive line, but now he's into a kind of self-help guru speaking, his forehead beaded with perspiration.

Then six more people enter the room: an assembly line of baggy white dress shirts and long ties knotted tight; hair slicked back with extra firm hold grease.

Jim introduces Vinny, who takes the podium.

Here's the deal, Vinny says. This is a door-to-door operation. Windows, siding and roofing. That's what we sell.

It's hot in the room and now I've started to sweat. I check my watch; it's 8:46 a.m.

I wonder about Missy, what she's doing right now. I picture her sitting on a couch, painting her toenails exotic colors. Then lighting a cigarette off an electric burner on a stovetop. I picture her in a bedroom in sexy underwear. Missy in her black bra and panties, posing in front of a mirror. I can see her pierced navel, the tattoo on her stomach. She told me she got that tattoo after the abortion because she never wanted to have any kids. That was, she said, until we got back together.

Meanwhile, Vinny, he's telling us why we're here. The six of us sitting at the table, he says, we're *canvassers*. We go out on cold calls and bring our leads back to the closers. When a closer seals the deal, that's when we earn commission.

Do a good job, Vinny says, soon you'll be up here with us.

The guy sitting across from me, a fat man with a mustache, raises his hand. Vinny goes on talking for a minute before motioning for this guy to put down his arm.

There are four parts to canvassing, Vinny goes. When you knock on someone's door, the first words out of your mouth should have nothing to do with why you're really there.

You want to eliminate defense mechanisms.

Establish a rapport.

Control the conversation.

Never ask a question that can be answered yes or no.

At most houses you'll see something on the front porch you can use. An item that tells you something about the people who live there.

A bike, a fishing rod, some baby's toy.

Even if there's only a *plant* you say, "I was just admiring your lovely geraniums"—or whatever kind of plant it is.

You say, "I have a bit of a green thumb myself."

Vinny uncaps a dry-erase marker and starts to write on the board.

This is called the *curve*, he says, and writes.

Next you've got the *opening line*, which is easy because it's always the same: "I was just noticing you're in the market for permanent materials for the exterior of your home."

I look around the table: everyone's writing, jotting this down. Don't be specific.

Never say windows, siding, or roofing because even if it looks like they need one in particular, you want them to buy all three.

And trust me, Vinny says. They will. If you do this right, they'll practically beg you to take their money.

When I look at the board again, there are two columns of words. The column on the right reads:

COMMUNICATION

DIALOGUE

CONFIDENT

ENTHUSIASTIC

POSITIVE

The one on the left gives the four parts to canvassing Vinny's been talking about: the curve, the opening line, the story and the appointment. At the moment, he's still talking about the appointment, which is the canvasser's endgame.

As for what the story is, I must have missed it.

25 OUTSIDE, IN THE PARKING LOT, CLOSERS STAND TOGETHER SMOKING MARLBOROS IN THEIR OVERSIZED HILFIGER SHIRTS AND PLAYING WITH their Zippos. Someone's cell phone rings. They all reach down to check the cell phones clipped to their belts. I check my watch

and notice it's stopped working. According to my watch, it's still 8:46 a.m.

Sitting in a Crown Victoria, I'm trapped in back next to the fat guy with the mustache. Vinny's behind the wheel, another white shirt rides up front.

Before you reach into another man's fridge, Vinny says, you ask permission.

He gets out and disappears into a police station.

The guy on my right turns to me, gut bulging over the seatbelt strapped tight across his lap. Eminem's playing on the radio.

Before you shit in another man's toilet, make sure it flushes, I go.

There's an empty Dunkin' Donuts cup on the floor between my feet. A matchbook from a strip club called the Catwalk.

Vinny walks out of the concrete station and slides a permit over his visor. I don't even know what town we're in. East Haven maybe. White noise from the car's speakers gives me a headache.

The car parked at the dead end of a cul-de-sac, Vinny and the guy sitting shotgun inside with the windows up, smoking a joint, I walk circles on the paved road, breathing in saltwater air.

When the closers finish their hot-box session, they get out arms stretched high like goal posts.

Following their footsteps toward the first house on the block, my fat friend tells me he used to smoke a little reefer in college—at Saint Olaf College in Minnesota, which is where he's from.

Already, I had him pegged as a Jackie Gleason-type, so from now on he's Minnesota Fats. He leans in close, his boozy breath hot on my face.

At the first two houses no one comes to the door, which is what you'd expect in a neighborhood where people leave for work. Plus, all the houses look like they were built yesterday, so I can't see anyone falling for this scam. But then again, here I am . . . not even getting paid.

Third time's a charm, Vinny goes, and he's right because now I can hear footsteps on the stairs inside.

The door opens the length of the chain and a man in a Hugh Hefner robe peers out like he's waiting on someone special. Schedules an appointment just to get us off his porch.

The door closes and Vinny shows me his grin like the guy's agreed to wire a cool million to the Swiss bank account of his choosing.

You see? It's that easy.

When it's our turn to try, me and Fats, we're on the poor side of town. The Fat Man, he waddles behind me, drinking from a flask, trying to keep up. The closers working the other end of the street, we're supposed to meet them somewhere in the middle.

I look at the houses around us, the burial plot yards of grass. I'm looking for items I can use:

I was just noticing your beware of dog sign.

Your broken television.

Your oozing refrigerator.

I was just admiring the dead cat rotting on your porch.

First door I knock on, the woman who answers doesn't speak any English. Or maybe that's what she wants us to think. I don't know.

Then we're greeted by a kid in Superman pajamas who says his parents aren't home. He's dragging the kind of tarp you'd wrap a body in for a cape. Blue tarp covers half a room like a tent. I hear an argument going on somewhere in the house: the sound of glass breaking, a suitcase, maybe, tumbling down the stairs. From inside a woman shouts CLOSE THAT GODDAMNED DOOR, and the kid, he raises an arm in a pose that could mean Superman or Hitler.

At the next house, this guy appears framed in the doorway wearing a helmet. He tells us about his head injury; his brain was so swollen doctors had to remove a piece of his skull. He says they sawed off the top of his head and kept the bone inside his stomach until the swelling went down. Now he's got a metal plate up there, but still he wears the helmet for protection.

Trying to shake the last drop from his whiskey flask, the Fat Man says he thought this would be easy. He tells me he worked in sales for years and once upon a time he could sell anything to anyone. Then his wife left him—the dirty bitch—his daughter's a lesbian who won't speak to him and he just learned he's got this fucking heart condition. He curses through his whole life story, which I call *Death of a Fucking Salesman*.

Meanwhile, all the rejection is starting to take its toll. I mean, I'm starting to take it personally.

Walking down the steps of every porch, I feel like I missed my line. Like I let down the team. Like I got shot down by the ugliest girl in the bar.

The next door slams in my face. It's like I just ruined Christmas. Fats, he tells me not to take it so hard. He knows how it is when you're not worth two minutes of someone's time. You have to let it go, move on to the next.

Besides, we're in the wrong place. In this place, Fats says, you can't sell shit. This is where people know there's no such thing as permanent material.

An old man holding an oxygen tank answers the door. He seals the valve on the canister and lights a cigarette. Says that he likes to live dangerously.

Those fucking towelheads that attacked us, the Fat Man goes, they're gonna get what's coming.

The trees on the street all look dead and my watch still says 8:46.

Hello, I was just noticing your roof's caving in.

The girl on the porch draws hard on her cigarette, burning away the paper. At the end of the butt's an inch of ash; I have the urge to flick it away. In this neighborhood, everybody smokes. That's why tobacco companies don't care about putting warnings on the packs. In this place, people know you can't die twice.

Come in, the girl says. Come in and we'll talk about the roof.

The screen door slaps behind us.

Fats waiting outside with his empty flask . . . I can see him through a dusty window. He looks smaller out there, like through the wrong end of a telescope.

In here, there's an air mattress in the middle of the living room. The girl doesn't sit down so much as collapses onto it. She pats for me to sit next to her. All around the bed, pots and pans filled with rainwater.

On the floor: a condom wrapper torn wide open.

I'm thinking about setting up an appointment for Vinny just as a joke.

Reclining on her air mattress, the girl, she says I look familiar. She's seen me somewhere before. Or my picture maybe.

She's got curly black hair, pale face with dark circles around her eyes. Her body type's what you'd call athletic . . . except that's a hypodermic needle sticking out of the stained lime green carpet.

I'm making my escape when the girl says wait, come back. She wants to know if my mother teaches high school in New Haven. She had my mother for English. She remembers there was this picture of me on the desk. Plus, she says, I look like her, my mother. Not that I look like a woman, but I know what she means.

I study the girl's face, trying to figure how long it's been since she dropped out.

And now she's showing me her pictures like I'm supposed to recognize something:

This is me with my niece.

Here's one of me at prom.

This was me two years ago before I got hooked on drugs.

She shuffles the stack and wraps it in rubber band; slides it back inside the envelope it was stuffed in.

I stare out the window, but Fats has disappeared.

The girl, she says, once upon a time, my mom was really a positive influence on her. She tells me her name, and I should say she says hello.

If I mention this to my mother, I'll have to tell her why I'm here. Wherever here is.

As I exit the house I see the Crown Vic parked out front, Fats in the back of the car like a perp who's just been arrested. I walk around to the driver's side, climb in next to the Fat Man, and Vinny goes, Ready?

IN THE PARKING LOT OF THE CORPORATE PARK I DISCOVER I'VE LOCKED MY KEYS INSIDE MY CAR. I CAN SEE MY I ♥ NY KEYCHAIN DANGLING from the ignition. The passenger's window's cracked, rolled down a couple inches, but I can't fit my arm through to reach the lock on the side of the door. I grip the window and pull

26

down but it won't budge and all of a sudden I'm wishing I had AAA.

I take a few steps back and give a sort of spinning side kick to the glass but nothing. I've wasted the whole day and now I'm stuck here with no one to call. Kicking a rotten apple with each step, I walk to the construction site across the street.

Here it's quitting time. Workers deposit equipment in flatbeds like a commercial for Ford trucks. They look at me expectantly, like I'm some kind of messenger. I walk over to two guys, ask if they have any tools that might be useful. I'm asking for advice.

The police? one of them says.

And the other one laughs out smoke.

Then I see it: part of a broken cinder block in roughly the shape of a football. I pick it up.

You're gonna go through it? the smoker says.

I nod and walk back to my car. I try hitting the window with the block of cement. It bounces and lands on my foot. I try again with similar results. I'm limping now, but at least there aren't any witnesses.

At some point, I realize I picked the wrong window. The fact that the window's partially open means it's more resistant. It gives a little with the force of each blow.

Block in hand, I drop back like a quarterback and let it fly. There's a terrific explosion; glass in all directions. I taste dust like sand from an hourglass in my mouth.

I approach the car, reach in, and unlock the door. Use the piece of cinder block to knock away the remaining shards, then drive across the street and return it to the site.

Driving home I have this crazy idea that this is hell and I died in the terrorist attacks two days ago . . . and there's this whole other life I can't remember. In that life, I would've gone to New York right out of college. I might have worked at the World Trade Center. I could have been a clerk for a law office or a janitor. In my other life, I could have been anyone.

Back at my parents' house, I find a package addressed to me from Missy. It's the pictures from our night out in the city. There's a card that reads *I thought you should have these, considering*.

I pick up the phone and dial her number but she doesn't answer.

THE NOTE FROM MISSY, IT SAYS IF ANYTHING SHOULD EVER HAPPEN TO HER, HER DAUGHTER SHOULD COME AND FIND ME IN NEW HAVEN.

27

Her daughter Emma.

The note's addressed to Emma. The handwriting, it's the same as on the card. Same as on the napkin, seven years ago.

So let me get this straight, I say.

We're inside the apartment now. In the living room. When I lived at home, my parents, they called it a "family room." The girl, she's sitting on the couch.

I say, Missy—your mother—left a note—

Yes, on the kitchen table.

Saying if anything should *happen* to her?

Yes.

And she hasn't been home since then?

The girl nods. Says she waited three days before leaving. She's been on a bus for the last eight hours, but Missy, she's still not answering her phone.

Has anyone called the police? I ask. Have you reported your mother missing?

I didn't . . . I didn't know what to do.

In the phonebook now, I'm looking up Social Services. I'm looking up DCF. The girl, now she's crying. Says her mother runs off all the time. For two or three days. But the note, it scared her. She says she didn't even know she *had* a father. She says her mother told her I was dead.

A car accident.

A terrorist attack.

Apparently, Missy thought up many different ways of killing me. Never remembered what the last one was.

But look here.

A birth certificate.

There's your name: _____.

In the space provided for *father*.

And I'm listed in the phonebook.

Emma, she says it wasn't that hard to find me.

Meanwhile, she's got this look now like it's Christmas morning and I'm thinking, Christ, if this girl is my daughter, look at all the years I've missed.

Birthdays. Holidays. First days of school.

Hold it.

(. . .)

If this girl is my daughter, this isn't the whole story. It can't be. It's all just a bit too rehearsed.

The note.

The birth certificate.

The crazy stripper mother.

If only she didn't look so much like me.

28

ACCORDING TO HER BIRTH CERTIFICATE, EMMANUELLE MAY WAS BORN IN JANUARY OF 1996 IN BANGOR, MAINE. FOUR MONTHS BEFORE I GRADUATED from college.

I lived with Missy in Vermont during the spring semester of my junior year and she returned to Maine in May of 1995.

I do the math. I count: May, June, July, August, September, October, November, December, January. I count off nine fingers and the only one left folded down is a pinky. Technically, thumbs aren't fingers—but you get the idea.

If she'd conceived in April, chances are, Missy didn't know she was pregnant when she left.

The real question, though, is *How could I have let this happen?*

In other words, how could I have gotten the same girl pregnant twice?

Over a period of two years.

Without trying.

Then again, maybe I had been trying.

Go down to planned parenthood—eighteen years old and you're sitting in the waiting room with your pregnant girlfriend, with all the other couples and teenage girls, and no one's making eye contact.

The pamphlets fanned out on the table in front of you.

Everyone subdued. Shamed. Stigmatized.

The specter of disease.

The pro-life protesters picketing outside the clinic. No windows on the building, so they can't see inside. A concrete fortress.

This is abortion day.

The first time Missy took the test, she took it in front of me and it came back negative.

Next time, the nurse at the clinic comes into the room, waving the test like a thermometer, and she gives us the results.

Missy puts the tips of her fingers to her mouth. Her heart-shaped lips. Pink lipstick, and the nail polish matches.

This is an after-school special.

This shit's emotionally scarring.

This is a big dose of reality for a summer home from college.

IT DOESN'T OCCUR TO ME UNTIL I SEE THE BIRTH CERTIFICATE, BUT Missy named her daughter after the baby we never had.

I ask myself: Why would she do this?

A constant, painful reminder.

On the other hand, maybe I've got it all wrong. The name, maybe it means a second chance.

I look at Emma, sitting on my couch.

Emma.

Emma May.

Emmanuelle.

What do you say to any twelve-year-old girl?

Come on, I say. We're going to the airport.

Why?

I have to pick up someone.

Who?

I have to pick up Norman.

And she says, Who's Norman?

This is so not good.

IN JUNE OF 2002 I MOVE TO MANHATTAN TO ATTEND NEW YORK FILM ACADEMY. I'D THOUGHT ABOUT FILM SCHOOL SINCE COLLEGE . . . BUT IT ALWAYS seemed like the sort of thing I was destined to regret not doing. Now I'm twenty-seven years old and my life is going nowhere. I've never held down a respectable job. I haven't been involved in a serious relationship since Missy. And the last time I saw her, before our walk in Central Park, she told me I reminded her of that character from *Great Expectations*.

So—I take out some student loans and move into a closet-size studio downtown.

First week I'm there, my next-door neighbor, he says do I know how come the rent's so cheap? He tells me the guy who lived here before me just left town after spending a weekend tied to a bed for crystal meth. Found out he's got HIV and his family, they wanted to sublet the place pretty fast.

He says, Welcome to the building. New York, he says like I don't know.

Meanwhile, the apartment's in a convenient location. There's a liquor store on the block and bars in every direction. I walk to the

JASON RAPCZYNSKI | 65

bars and shops in the neighborhood, but I'm afraid of getting lost and it's a month before I risk the subway.

That summer, when I'm supposed to be looking for a job, I drink each night from five o'clock until five in the morning. During the first few hours of drinking I work on a screenplay. I write until eight or nine o'clock, then go out to the bars. When the bars close I sit down at my computer, open a bottle, and enter the chat rooms. The next day I always have a few new screen names on my buddy list, but I hardly ever recall what they said. On a few occasions I meet a girl online, and then in person the very same night or morning. When I stop drinking, I delete my entire list.

30

I MEET NORMAN IN THE FALL, DURING MY FIRST WORKSHOP AT NYFA. "WRITING THE SCREEN-PLAY." THE CLASS IS FILLED WITH MOVIE BUFFS WHO KNOW all the lines to their favorite films. They plan to hit big, move out to L.A. and be millionaires. But first they have to learn about plot points, the inciting incident, and how to write a ninety-page script.

The course is taught by Rick Dean, a Hollywood guru type who's published three editions of his book *How to Write Your Screenplay*. In the second edition, he changed the title to *Dean on Screen*.

Dean's made a good living selling the rights to half a dozen movie scripts. His screenplays are optioned by major studios and production companies.

Paramount.

Zoetrope.

Miramax.

But nothing he writes is ever filmed.

"Greenlight status," he calls it.

The first thing you learn about Dean is, he speaks the language of the industry.

On the second night of the workshop, students pick the class-mates they want to read from the first ten pages of their scripts. Norman picks me to be one of his readers, but I only have to speak about six lines.

Norman's a big guy, heavyset with wild, curly hair. Wears thick horn rims low on his nose . . . a very intense, penetrating look.

The lines I have to read, the character is Satan.

After class ends, Norman, he asks if anyone wants to go for a coffee. At first, no one says anything. Then someone comments on how he's had too much coffee already. I get up and walk down the hall as the class filters out of the room.

From inside the elevator, I can see the assembly line of students, moving down the hall. They swarm out of every doorway, filtering into a film school parade. Holding down the button on the panel, I listen to the music as elevator doors close just ahead of the crowd.

WHEN I SPOT NORMAN ON THE SIDEWALK AFTER CLASS, I TELL HIM GOOD WORK.

I tell him, "Realistic dialogue." I tell him I'm liking his script.

Do you wanna get a coffee? he asks.

And I say, Howbout we grab a beer?

At the bar we talk about movies, literature, our favorite books. We talk about the screenplays that we're working on. Norman, for some reason, he refuses to call movies *films*.

Norman, he tells me some of the best work he's ever seen was originally shot as home video.

The birthday party with the frightening clown.

The trampoline accident in the backyard.

The Christmas morning kids find out there's no such thing as Santa.

It's the wrapping paper, Norman says. It's always the wrapping paper. Parents too cheap or stupid to buy a separate roll for Santa's gifts.

The parents, he says they need to have a separate roll. Or maybe he means *role* as in *part*. And I don't know, maybe he's talking about himself. Maybe he's talking about his own personal childhood traumas.

For a while, Norman tells me about how there's no such thing as reality television. He says, shows may be made to give the *illusion* of reality, condensed into a neat little facsimile, but life—real life!—moves along a timeline, not a narrative arc.

In real life, there's no time out for commercials.

In real life, everything's a commercial. All of it. Anything that's not considered art. We live in a world of product placement.

The Louis Vuitton monogrammed handbag.

The baseball cap with the logo of your favorite team.

Even what we choose to read in public.

Norman, he says he wouldn't be caught dead reading back issues of monthly magazines in the waiting room of his dentist's office.

GQ.

Esquire.

Vanity Fair.

In real life, plot points never happen when they're supposed to.

In real life, you don't know what the inciting incident is until later on.

Norman, he always takes the jackets off the books that he reads in public. Wraps them in brown paper like how you covered your textbooks in grade school. Plain brown wrappers like how they used to sell pornography. In public, this is how he reads.

In restaurants and coffee shops.

While sitting alone in bars.

Norman reads in Washington Square Park, and sitting between the marble lions in front of the New York Public Library.

He takes out books on subway cars, even when he's standing.

If I'm going to take the time to read, Norman says, I want to *become* the story.

I picture him sitting at home making book covers. Scotch tape. Scissors. A roll of plain brown wrapping paper. Brown paper rolled and wrapped in cellophane.

The extra paper, Norman says, he uses it to make his own insulating sleeves. Covers half the cup when he takes out his coffee from Starbucks.

He lifts his glass to drink. Thick glasses slide down the bridge of his nose. "It's My Life" plays in the bar where we're sitting.

Great books make the reader write, Norman says. The great works make the audience work—to contribute their own meanings. If this is the proper function of literature, how does that translate to film? Which raises the question: who's the real *maker* of a film?

The screenwriter?

The director?

The actors?

Is it the camera?

If a work of art must be *experienced*, what role does the audience play?

Do great movies inspire viewers to act?

To direct?

Do they inspire life to imitate art?

If life and art are also the same, Norman says, which is the imitation?

32

BEFORE LONG WE'RE BOTH PRETTY DRUNK AND NORMAN SAYS IF I DRINK WITH HIM THE REST OF THE NIGHT HE'LL PICK UP ALL THE TABS.

Next place we go, it's this swank blue neon lounge with a dress code. The bouncer, he instructs me to remove my baseball cap . . . I take it off and we're let inside—but sitting at the bar, I put the hat back on.

The bartender comes over right away. Thin in a black dress and dark from tanning; she has dark hair and sharp features. She tells me to lose the hat.

I place it on the bar and we order.

The bartender leaves, I put the hat back on, and she comes back with the drinks.

I thought I told you to take that thing off . . .

She's angry now, but she looked that way to begin with. It's a Red Sox cap and, in New York, that can start a fight.

Norman drinks his gin and tonic down fast and orders another.

He orders another one for me too. I drink the one I still have and we drink the next round fast.

Another.

Not long after that Norman's speaking only in German. On the subway, he met a German girl and had a conversation with her in that language, and when the bartender comes over again, he orders drinks in German.

Are you speaking English? she asks.

Nein!

I order the drinks.

Norman, he drinks his and motions for another.

The bartender sets it down and walks away, but he follows her to the end of the bar.

What the hell are you saying? she shouts.

I try to bring him back to his seat but it's too late. The bouncer comes and kicks him out.

He's got to sign for the tab, the bartender says.

I go to the door and call him back.

Norman stumbling around on the sidewalk. He comes inside and examines the credit receipt. I can see he's trying to figure out the tip. Doing the math.

As he scribbles something and signs the slip, tearing the paper, I notice that our drinks are still on the bar. I finish mine and then I drain his too. Then we start walking.

Norman lives in a two-bedroom near the East Village. When we get to his apartment we have to be very quiet, on account of his roommate. I wait in his room while he goes to get the beers. He's in the kitchen a long time before he returns.

I think she's asleep, he says, meaning his roommate.

Hands me a bottle.

After that he lights a big cigar and starts talking. More coherent now, but I'm at my limit. I look around the room. There are no decorations of any kind. No posters or pictures or shelves. The whole room looks white, freshly painted and bare as empty space.

Norman's still talking, but it's difficult to focus on what he's saying. Then his voice changes and he's saying something about me, and he says, If you use any of this against me, I'll kill you.

Really, I have no idea.

I'd better get going now, I say. And put my bottle down on his desk.

Then I'm walking through the living room, up stairs and down a hallway until I reach an exit and, passing through the big heavy doors, I make my way out into the cool damp early morning on Houston Street.

33

THE FOLLOWING WEEK, AFTER WORKSHOP, WE HEAD DOWN TO KGB. NOT LONG AFTER WE ARRIVE, NORMAN INTRODUCES ME TO A POET WHO LOOKS like a young Gary Snyder.

This kid, he's got a long beard and a ponytail, a necklace bearing some sort of Native symbol. After a few rounds, he produces his chapbook from a shoulder bag and I begin leafing through the poems.

I read one of them out loud, and he buys us a round. I read another one. The poems, they're all about nature and wilderness, how we're killing the planet. I like them better the more I drink.

After that Norman suggests that the three of us visit a strip club.

I say I'd rather get something for my money, and the poet says he doesn't see anything wrong with visiting a prostitute even though he's got an Asian girlfriend waiting at home. Then I tell Norman about the club in Maine where Missy may still work and he says, Well, fuck it, let's go *there*.

We head out looking for another dive. A few blocks later I see the sign:

DANCING! COCKTAILS!
OPEN TIL 4 A.M. EVERY NITE

Inside, the bartender takes one look at Norman's drunk ass and says, Are you *kidding* me? He can't be in here like that.

I say, Come on, man, he'll just sit quietly with a glass of water.

Next thing I know, I'm at the bar having my drinks paid for by a transvestite named Sherri. Sherri wears a plaid skirt with leather straps and buckles, fishnet stockings, a black wig.

Sherri has freckled shoulders, a pierced tongue.

Glasses like librarians wore in 1960.

It gets to be two o'clock, 2:15, 2:30.

I have no idea what happened to the poet.

Sherri and I put Norman in a cab and get into one of our own.

UNFORTUNATELY, I DON'T PAY ANY ATTENTION TO HOW LONG the ride is or where the driver's taking us or what floor her unit's on—but inside, the place looks like an old-school porn palace with leopard-print rugs, leather couches, tanks of exotic fish.

Then Sherri leads me into the bedroom to meet her gender-bending roommate, a fat man with enormous breast implants—spread across a bed with a canopy, all Victoria's Secret and stroking a black cat.

In the living room, I remove my jacket and sit down on the couch. After a few minutes, the roommate comes out of the bedroom and flashes his enormous sagging breasts.

When we're alone again, Sherri takes hits of crack from a makeshift pipe made from aluminum foil and a plastic Diet Coke bottle.

Cracked out, s/he unzips and shows me some cock, which hangs enormous, uncircumcised and unshaved.

---

34   OUTSIDE, I HAVE NO IDEA WHERE THE FUCK I AM. IT'S A COOL MORNING AND I LEFT MY JACKET BACK AT SHERRI'S PLACE. I WANDER AROUND DRUNK for a while before stumbling onto a main road. The city skyline is nowhere in sight.

After a few minutes, a bus comes by and somehow I manage to flag it down. I have exactly two dollars in my pocket, just enough for the fare.

Sitting at the front of the bus, I watch the lines blur as they pass below, yellow and white. There are a few other people on board, all spread out. They look as if they might come alive at any moment.

Airport, the driver says.

The airport's the last and only stop.

Inside JFK I find an ATM, insert my card, and enter the PIN. The receipt indicates a negative balance. The subway isn't running for some reason and I've got no money for a cab.

I find a payphone, dial a calling card number, and call my parents' house in Connecticut. It's after 4 a.m. and my father answers the phone. I tell him I'm stranded at the airport and in need of some cash at once.

Have you been drinking? he asks.

Don't be ridiculous . . .

After that, I pass out on the floor beneath the payphone, and next thing I know, there's a police officer kicking at my feet. He tells me to find a bench, so I look around and find one. When I wake up, I use my Metro Pass to take the subway . . . fall asleep on the train . . . and open my eyes just in time for my stop.

In my apartment I go straight to bed and sleep for most of the day.

I decide I'd better quit drinking for a while after that.

EMMA, SHE'S LOOKING OVER AT ME FROM THE PASSENGER'S SEAT OF MY CAR. 35

Buckle up, she says as we merge onto I-95.

Usually, I always wear my seatbelt.

Windows down, I accelerate onto the Q Bridge, past a billboard advertising laser eye surgery. In the left lane an 18-wheeler screams past, picture of a smiling pig on its rear door, the logo of a gourmet food distributor, smiling like a dead cartoon.

Breathing in saltwater air, I look out at the harbor, spread like an oil spill toward the swirling horizon.

Almost there, I go.

TOWARD THE END OF MY FIRST SEMESTER AT NYFA I GO OUT LOOKING TO MEET SOME PEOPLE —

It must be a weekday, since all the bars I look in are fairly deserted, and I walk up and down the city looking in through plate glass windows.

After a while, I look in one where there's a girl sitting alone at the bar. I figure she's with someone, so I scope out a few other places, but when I return she's still alone. Pulling open the heavy door, I'm greeted by a rush of warm air from inside.

When I get up to the bar, I recognize this girl from somewhere. Then it occurs to me: she was sitting next to me on the subway this morning. What are the chances?

I just saw you on the subway, I tell her.

We talk for a while and she tells me she's new in town. We drink and she tells me about this guy she's trying to get over. The story goes, she only knew him for a week, met him when she came here over the summer to look at apartments. She tells me she's a waitress at this bar on the Bowery, and maybe I'd like to stop by.

Her name's Lucy, by the way.

Lucy from Houston, Texas.

WE MAKE PLANS TO GO OUT THE FOLLOWING NIGHT . . . AND THE next day I'm working on my screenplay when Norman calls.

I'm heading over to the library, he says. Can I stop by on the way over?

Sure. What are you going for?

Research.

For your movie?

Some of it.

Norman's been working on his screenplay for several months,

but he hasn't spoken of it very often. All I know is the main character's Plague and it has something to do with the Four Horsemen of the Apocalypse. I don't know if this is supposed to be a comedy or what. But that's Norman for you.

Ten minutes later he's standing outside my building. I come down and let him in.

That reminds me, I say once we're inside my apartment. I have some books that are overdue.

Which ones?

Those over there.

He examines the stack of library books on my desk, picks up each one, and restacks them in reverse order.

Would you mind dropping those off for me? At the library.

Norman, he looks down, laughs, and adjusts his glasses with an index finger.

Well, I haven't been *totally* honest with you, he says. I'm actually on my way to a bar.

So?

I'm going for Eight-Minute Dating.

He nods.

Well, then, let's have a drink.

I walk into the kitchen and remove a fifth of vodka from the freezer. Wash, rinse and dry two glasses.

You want olives?

No, only in a martini. This is good vodka and I like to taste it.

I remove a jar of olives from the refrigerator, uncap it and remove an olive with a fork, bite the olive off the fork and raise my glass.

We touch glasses.

Saluda, Norman says, and drinks four ounces of vodka in one swallow.

I drink mine down halfway, then finish it off with another olive.

Another hit? Norman says.

And I say, Sure.

After that I tell Norman I'll call him later. I say maybe we'll meet up.

Then I go out and walk to the subway stop where I'm supposed to be meeting Lucy.

37 I GET THERE EARLY SO I HEAD FOR THE MCDONALD'S UNDER THE SCAFFOLDING ACROSS THE STREET. EXCEPT FOR THE OLIVES, I HAVEN'T EATEN anything all day and the vodka's having its effect. I order two McChickens and French fries and I eat it all in about five minutes. Then I walk back across the street.

Hello.

Nice timing, Lucy says.

Just came from getting her nails done and now she's showing them to me. Holding both hands out for me to see. The nails, they're long and pink.

You like?

Nice, I say. So what do you feel like doing?

Lucy, she wants to try this restaurant called Tao.

Midtown.

Fabulous.

She wants to know, have I heard of it?

We walk down to the platform and wait for a train. When the

train comes, we stand for the first two stops and when two seats open up, we sit down.

After that I don't feel much like talking and Lucy looks at me and smiles in the fluorescent light.

Tell me something, she says. Tell me about your day.

Well, my friend stopped by. We had a few drinks.

Oh, really, what time was that?

An hour ago, maybe. He was on his way to some kind of dating function.

Really? What does it involve?

Apparently, you sit at a table with someone for eight minutes and find out things about that person before moving on to someone else. It's called Eight-Minute Dating. He's done it before.

Any luck?

None yet.

Well, maybe tonight will be different.

THE TRAIN STOPS AND WE GET OFF AT 53RD
STREET. WALK UP MADISON AVENUE.

Tao's this real hip place, Asian Fusion, with a sixteen-foot statue of Buddha on the first floor. The place was once a balconied movie theater and, before that, a stable for the Vanderbilt family. It's located at 42 East 58th Street. Now, once again, this venue caters to the elite.

Somehow we end up with a table up in the Skybox and I look down at the sea of people already eating their meals.

Tourists and socialites.

Good wine.

Expensive dinners.

Already, I'm wondering how I'm going to pay for this.

In order to receive a loan refund, I'm only taking two courses at NYFA. My student loan covers the cost of three courses per semester, and the cost of one course is equal to my rent for the duration of one semester. Since I don't have a job, I've run up the balance on my credit card, while my diet has consisted primarily of eggs and microwaveable burritos.

I study the menu.

Arrange my silverware.

Drape the cloth napkin across my lap as our waiter approaches the table.

Our waiter is quite fat and has a ponytail. He talks for a long time in an effeminate, quirky manner, recommending many things. He recommends that we order all of our courses at once so they'll be ready at even intervals.

He recommends wines paired with foods.

The most expensive dishes on the menu.

Already, he's recommending desserts.

Dressed all in black with seashell buttons on his Chinese-collared shirt; his face sweats misdirected tears.

Sweat stains extra dark under his arms.

After he leaves, I go, I'm going to use the bathroom.

When I return, Lucy, she's looking out over the crowd.

Look, there, she says. See that blonde. I think that's Paris Hilton. Wait, she wouldn't be sitting down *there*.

See that man.

See those girls.

That guy over there, Lucy says, I think that he plays for the Rangers.

I look at the guy and she could mean baseball or hockey.

Out come the Newports and Lucy fires up a cigarette.

Lucy smokes despite the fact that she's a long-distance runner. She actually chain smokes, and I do my best to keep up. She takes breaks to smoke before each course, and this is before the smoking ban, back when you could still pollute the air and ruin people's dinners.

This wasn't supposed to be dinner, though—just drinks—which is why I stopped at McDonald's.

But I don't tell Lucy that I've already eaten until after the food has arrived.

After that she tells me this story about how she once made a date to have dinner with someone at a restaurant she'd really been looking forward to trying, but when her date showed up he said he'd already eaten.

And that was a real turn off, she says. Not that *this* is a date.

Lucy, she could almost pass for Sarah Jessica Parker.

Sarah Jessica circa 1993.

Sarah Jessica Parker costarring in *Striking Distance* with Bruce Willis.

Before the check arrives, Lucy tells me about the last guy she was out with.

I was at this bar, she says, the other day . . . and I made plans to go running with the bartender.

She draws deeply on her cigarette.

So we go for a run—only about two miles—and all of a sudden he says, "Well, this is it." And I say, Wait . . . but I can see now we're at his *apartment* building and he's already starting to make his way inside. "You can come up and use my shower," he says. And I'm thinking does he really expect me to say yes? Then he asks me if I'd like to at least come in for some *water*. Do you believe that?

Unbelievable, I say.

I know!

You can shower here, baby.

I know! Where does he get off?

And I say, Good question.

39

OUT ON THE SIDEWALK NOW AND A VOICE CALLS OUT FROM SOMEWHERE BEHIND US. WE'RE UPTOWN, WALKING TOWARD THE PARK.

Lucy stops and turns around.

Two girls: dressed to kill and both very attractive.

I stand aside and watch the three of them interact.

A ringtone plays: one of the girls moves aside to take the call.

A few minutes later, Lucy and I, we move on.

I don't believe this, Lucy says. I'm weak in the knees.

So you're into girls?

No, that girl is *roommates* with the guy I told you about.

The one-week guy?

Yes!

Which girl?

Not the one on the cell phone.

I see.

I don't know why I feel this way, Lucy says. I mean, that happened over the summer.

And you only knew him a week?

Yes! I just don't understand it. But I felt that we really *connected*.

Well, people have been known to fall in love at first sight. A week's nothing to be ashamed of.

But that's just it. I wasn't in *love* with him. I just don't feel any closure.

I can understand that.

I mean, we talked on the phone the entire time I was back in Texas. Then when I finally moved up here he said he couldn't see me anymore because he had a girlfriend and he didn't want to be tempted. I don't know, maybe he had a girlfriend the whole time.

It's possible. Then again, you did spend a whole week together.

Maybe she was away.

That would be convenient.

What?

Never mind.

Anyhow, Lucy says. I know this isn't something I should be talking about on a first date.

WE END UP HEADING FOR THE BAR NORMAN'S AT. IN THE CAB, LUCY remembers how I told her about Eight-Minute Dating, and now, all of a sudden, she wants to go.

She wants to see what types of people are there.

No one unusual, I tell her. But she wants to see for herself.

When we get there Norman's very drunk. The dating game has ended and he's cocked off his ass.

I'm buying! he says. And we sit down at the bar, the three of us, with Lucy in the middle.

I'm thinking, Well, at least he's got money.

After a few more drinks I suggest that I do the ordering from now on, since the bartenders are clearly sick of dealing with Norman, but by this point he's unable to distinguish between the concepts of *ordering* and *paying*.

I'm buying the drinks! he insists.

Meanwhile, he's also talking to Lucy, trying to build me up.

This guy right here, he is the MOST HONEST person I know. If he's thinking something, he'll tell you.

Lucy laughs.

And *he* is going to be a GREAT FILMMAKER!

I stop listening at some point, or try to anyway, but Norman keeps going on about me.

A few minutes later, when Lucy turns to me, he thinks she's questioning his sincerity. His head's tilted at this ridiculous angle, almost parallel to the bar, and he's listening intently to what she's saying. His eyes look enormous behind the thick lenses of his glasses. He looks pretty much insane.

A moment later, she turns back to him.

And all of a sudden: AND HE DOESN'T USE CONDOMS!

I nearly spill my beer. Lucy, she's cracking up. And now Norman's trying to recover, insisting that my ex-girlfriend Missy was somehow responsible for getting pregnant when we were both eighteen.

His *ex*-girlfriend, Norman says, wouldn't let him use a condom.

This is what I get for writing an autobiographical script.

This is what I get for trying to make my life into a movie.

I turn to the one of the bartenders and she hears this, too: Check, please!

40

AFTER THAT THE THREE OF US END UP HEAD-
ING OVER TO THE ROOSEVELT HOTEL.

Lucy, she's gotten her second wind and this was where she stayed when she first came here over the summer and now she wants to see it.

The place where she met the guy she hasn't gotten over.

We're here to revisit her past.

To find some closure.

So—the cab lets us off across the street and we head for the hotel entrance where a pair of flags flap in the wind.

We walk past the valets, the bellhops, the luggage carts. Follow Lucy through the doors . . . and I'm looking up at the high-domed ceiling of the Art Deco lobby.

After a round at the lobby bar, I go outside to get some air and I'm followed by a blonde in a black dress. This woman, she has broad shoulders and there's something quite imposing about her.

She flicks the wheel of her lighter as if to announce her presence with fire.

I'm on an overnight business trip with my marketing team, she says.

And smokes.

Making these odd *whistling* sounds as she inhales on her cigarette.

I light one and smoke it and flick it out into the street.

Back inside, Lucy says she has something to tell me. What she tells me is, she wants to be just friends.

In the first place, I say, you're the one who said this was a date.

First it's not, and then it is. Now it's not again.

Lucy, she says, I just thought you'd appreciate my honesty.

I do. Appreciate it.

I say, Honesty's underrated.

When you're honest, you just hurt someone's feelings. Lie to protect someone and that's when you end up devastating people.

NOT LONG AFTER THAT IT'S LAST CALL IN THE LOBBY BAR, SO WE decide on another place.

I go over to the businesswoman and into her cell phone she's calling someone a "sissy."

Sissy, she says like a dominatrix.

When she's finished talking, I go, Are you going someplace else?

Well, that all depends, she says. You know somewhere we could go?

I know a place.

All right. Let me check with my team.

She goes over to a table where three well-dressed young men are sitting—the only other people in the bar.

They all look about my age.

Late twenties.

Very slick.

A moment later, the dominatrix, she comes back over to me.

OK, let's go.

Outside, she lights another cigarette and inhales the way she did before, sucking air through pursed lips.

What's up with that? I ask.

And she says, It's a sex thing.

AT THE NEXT PLACE, THE BARTENDER REFU-
SES TO SERVE NORMAN, SO I TELL HIM TO HAVE A
SEAT AT A TABLE. HE HANDS ME HIS CHECK CARD AND LUCY
sits down with him as I go up to order the drinks.

At the bar, one of the teammates asks me if I'm with Lucy. I look over at Lucy. The table's nearby and I see that she's listening.

No. We're not together.

Are you *sure* about that? another teammate says.

Pretty sure.

I think he's lying, the first one says.

And all of a sudden Norman starts laughing hysterically. Pointing at the teammates, he goes, Are you guys *sharks*?

I turn to look at the businesswoman.

The team leader.

The dominatrix.

She's sitting at the bar with the third team member—clean cut and he looks unsure.

They're facing one another and she's holding his hand in both of hers like she's about to read his palm. The way her legs are crossed, it makes her calf muscle appear extra big.

Then she starts moving one of her hands up this guy's forearm, running her fingernails lightly over his skin.

I ask for beers and then order some shots of whiskey.

The bartender pours the drinks.

RIGHT BEFORE NORMAN GETS KICKED OUT OF
THE BAR, THAT'S WHEN HE TELLS LUCY ABOUT HIS
BIG FEAR.

His "pedophilic phobia" is what he calls it. Not a fear *of* child molesters, but a fear of *becoming* one. Norman has OCD and one of his compulsions is to reveal this, his darkest fear, within about ten minutes of meeting someone at a bar.

It's the worst thing I can think of, he tells me, which is why I fear it. Becoming what people hate the most.

This sort of intimacy with anyone makes me uncomfortable, and the first time I heard this, my initial response was limited to something like *Well, I guess that's pretty fucked-up* . . . but while I don't fully understand the psychology of Norman's personality, I'm sure it has something to do with insecurity and alienation, his overbearing father, and the fact that he's a twenty-seven-year-old virgin.

But even apart from his disturbing obsession—which some people mistakenly call a *tendency*—Norman obviously has no social skills. He asks out just about every girl he meets and already his lecherous disposition has become notorious among fellow film students. Nevertheless, I like Norman—perhaps only in the way that I like all desperate people—and there seems to be no point in trying to avoid him.

LUCKILY, LUCY, SHE WAS A PSYCHOLOGY MAJOR.

He's great, she goes . . . as Norman flaps his arms wildly at a passing cab.

I say, Isn't he?

BACK DOWNTOWN, THE CAB LETS US OFF A FEW BLOCKS FROM EACH OF OUR APARTMENTS.

So . . . I say, turning to Lucy. You can come in and use my shower.

She laughs.

Goes, Well, maybe just for some *water*.

I turn to Norman.

He nods and sways.

We're all very drunk.

Well, my friend. This is where we go our separate ways.

THE SKYLINE IN MY REARVIEW MIRROR, I TAKE THE FIRST EXIT AFTER THE BRIDGE . . . TURN ONTO LIGHTHOUSE ROAD . . . AND WE'RE AT THE AIRPORT.

Follow the signs for short-term parking.

Emma, she's still sitting in the passenger's seat with a bag on her lap, looking out at a plane as it takes off from a runway. Out there, half the planes are corporate jets, parked nose-to-nose on the tarmac.

ExxonMobile.

Coca Cola.

Procter & Gamble.

The private jets of *Forbes* freaks who fly their prodigal offspring back to Yale at the start of each semester.

The prince from the country you've never heard of.

The brand-name cereal heiress.

I look over at Emma:

Pale skin branded with scars. Inscribed with initials scarred into her forearm.

The scar on her left forearm, it reads EM?

And we're rolling. Backwards. I pull the parking break. Look over at Emma:

The label on her backpack reads JanSport.

The word on her shirt, it says *Magic.*

Silver letters across the front of a black shirt, glittering.

On her watch, there's a picture of Mickey Mouse. Arabic numerals, a pink plastic band. Corporate vermin smiling on the face of a clock.

The way she's dressed, this seems intentionally ironic.

Wait here, I go, getting out of the car. And lock your door.

Emma's face lights up with a smile like I just made my first fatherly remark.

I snap the wheel of my Zippo and head for the terminal, smoking. Footsteps on the grainy asphalt. Gray sky like a padded ceiling overhead.

45 WALKING THROUGH A HALL OF WINDOWS, I FOLLOW THE SIGNS FOR ARRIVALS. AT THE END OF THE HALL, A ROOM LIKE A WAREHOUSE OFFICE.

To the right is a loading dock with a baggage slide and a row of movie theater chairs. Two quarter gumball machines and, inside, they say feed the children.

On the other side of the terminal is the rental car desk. Stations for Hertz, Budget, and Avis—and the signs displaying rates for each one.

There's an old school vending machine displaying an image of a lighthouse. Twelve-ounce soda cans inside.

A tower of yellow pages twenty phonebooks high beside the world's oldest surviving payphone.

For some reason, there's a display of brochures advertising Broadway musicals.

Brochures advertising local attractions.

The lights overhead, each one like a fixture removed from some interrogation room, buzz like insects.

I CHECK MY WATCH AND IT'S ABOUT THAT TIME. UP ON THE FLIGHT BOARD, ON TIME SWITCHES TO DELAYED. 46

Outside, behind the terminal, the back lot's landscaped like a miniature golf course with a row of carts parked alongside the high barbed-wire fence. I sit on a miniature bench and light a cigarette.

Overhead, the wooden control tower looks like giant tree-house—like a Disney World attraction.

Adventureland or Frontierland.

The Swiss Family Treehouse.

Standing at the fence that separates the parking lot from the airfield, I watch Norman's plane taxi along the runway as it arrives from Chicago.

BACK IN THE TERMINAL WHERE ARRIVING PASSENGERS IS PAINTED HIGH ABOVE A DOOR—THE KIND OF DOOR YOU SEE IN MOVIE PRISONS.

A keypad on one side, a bulletproof window.

Through the window, you see a stretch of hallway going around a corner.

You see white walls, industrial carpeting. The parade of passengers, arriving.

Stencil on the door, it says NO ENTRY and AUTHORIZED PERSONNEL ONLY.

It says, *For a good time call . . .* in pencil, but you can't read the rest.

I see Norman through the window in the door. Through the window he looks smaller, like through the wrong end of a telescope. Glass so thick and the door is huge and gray.

When it opens, he's first to come through.

NORMAN, HE LOOKS GOOD.

Says he lost a little weight.

Had the laser eye procedure.

Nine months sober and living on his own.

Next week, Norman says, he starts teaching community college.

I grab one of his bags as they land at the bottom of the metal slide. A leather travel bag that says "Gucci" on the label. The one he's holding, it has the monogram of Louis Vuitton. He picks up his carry-on and shoulders it. Says he's done with plain brown wrappers.

This isn't the Norman I remember. Last time I saw Norman, he was practically begging Reggie for a job.

FOR SOME REASON, I DON'T TELL NORMAN ABOUT EMMA BEFORE we get to the car.

Actually, it's more like I can't tell him.

Can't bring myself to say it.

I have this crazy idea that, if I say anything, she won't be there when we get back.

Like I've invented her.

Like this whole day so far has been a dream.

I don't really know what to make of this.

Except maybe it's a normal reaction.

Maybe it's how I'm supposed to be feeling.

Unsettled.

The rug pulled out from under me.

On the other hand, maybe I've got it all wrong.

Maybe it's the other way around.

Like if I mention Emma she *will* be there.

Waiting.

After all this time.

Then we're ten yards away from the car and my passenger's seat looks empty.

The runaway has run off. Disappeared. Fled the scene. Of course this would fucking happen.

A sinking feeling in the pit of my stomach like I just swallowed gum, I get out my cell phone with no one to call.

Hold out the phone like I'm trying to get a signal.

Pan around the parking lot.

The runway on the screen of my phone, that means I've got it set to *picture*.

And all of a sudden Norman goes, Who's that in your car?

For a minute I'm too distracted or relieved to ask Norman how he even knows which car is mine.

But there's Emma, sitting in the back.

She's moved to the backseat so my friend can sit up front with me.

She's done this on her own.

I don't know much about adolescents, but this kind of consideration doesn't seem to be a hallmark of your average twelve-year-old girl.

The car shakes as Norman collapses into the passenger's seat.

I introduce Emma.

My daughter, apparently.

Norman gives me this look like a raised eyebrow.

Then one like nothing I do surprises him.

Hello, he goes, reaching back his hand.

And to me: She looks just like you.

48

BACK AT MY APARTMENT: I DON'T KNOW WHERE ELSE TO GO AND I NEED TO COME UP WITH A PLAN.

My mother: out of the question.

But what other option is there?

I sit on the couch and think.

What the hell was I thinking?

Bringing both of them back here?

Or having Norman fly out for a visit in the first place?

Since leaving New York, I've only seen him once.

Two years ago.

When he drove all the way from his parents' house in Chicago.

When he spent four days drinking and hanging around Reggie.

Norman and Reggie together.

I won't make that mistake again.

A SHRIEK FROM THE KITCHEN . . . A CABINET SLAPS SHUT.

I get in there and Emma's got her hand covering her mouth in a pose that reminds me of Missy.

Gives me this horrified look like she's found a severed head in my freezer.

What happened?

Beat.

You have *maggots*!

What? Where?

She points to one of the cabinets beneath the granite counter and I open it.

What I'm looking at is a bag of rotted potatoes that have decomposed into a pool of sludge.

White worms swimming in black sludge like motor oil.

Off-white.

Light brown.

Larvae.

I've never seen maggots before . . . and what occurs to me is, if I discover this mess on my own, I probably have no idea what the hell I'm looking at.

I mean, I would have figured it out.

Eventually.

But when you see something for the first time, you don't always know what it is.

I INFLATE THE AIR MATTRESS IN MY SPARE BEDROOM . . . AND AFTER EMMA GOES OFF AND CLOSES THE DOOR, NORMAN AND I STAY UP FOR A WHILE, talking.

I tell him what's gone down and Norman, he wants to know where that leaves *him*.

He wants to know what the *plan* is. What we're going to do.

What do you mean *we*? I tell him.

I go, Sorry if this messed up your trip. But I have a responsibility here. At least, to figure something out.

I know, Norman says. Norman, he understands.

What he meant: What am I gonna do?

He wants to know how I'm feeling about all this.

And is there anything he can do to help?

After we're done talking—after Norman goes off to sleep in my bed and I drown the maggots in bleach—I stay up for a while longer, sitting on the couch between the bedrooms, the cherry of my cigarette glowing in the dark.

AT THE BEGINNING OF MY SECOND SEMESTER AT NYFA I MEET A GIRL AT A BAR IN THE VILLAGE.

Marissa's one of these "Tischies"—a film student at NYU—and she looks like one, dresses the way they dress. When we meet she's wearing all black with ripped fishnets . . . spikes and chains, piercings and tattoos. She says she's on her way to a club and I should meet her there. I decide to go.

After a few more drinks, I tell Norman we're going to this club, so we leave the bar and head on over. Out front's a cross-section of freaky and male glitz, silk shirt poster boys who never wait in line but stand in front of clubs outside roped-off sections of sidewalk—narrow, neon-lit cattle lanes of brass and red felt.

Inside, the place is a meat market: '80s music playing, people dancing to remixed '80s songs, bare skin everywhere. The TV screens overhead, they display closed-circuit images of the rave crowd in the club.

This one's a crane shot.

That one's a low angle.

That little red light, it means *record*.

Meanwhile, the people on screen, they don't even know they're on camera.

This is the kind of footage that will end up on the club's website.

Later, on the promoter's MySpace page.

Then on the bartender's Facebook.

Like everything else, this scene will end up on the Internet.

The shot girl walks by carrying a rack of glasses like test tubes on a tray. A guy wearing Speedos swoops down on a swing that hangs twenty feet from the ceiling. Back and forth, back and forth, high above the bar.

The word on his hat, it says *Lifeguard*.

On screen, the rave crowd dances. Strobe lighting gives the illusion of slow motion. This lighting, it can trigger seizures in cases of photosensitive epilepsy. It happens all the time; people have seizures in clubs.

Complex partial.

Simple partial.

Atonic.

When your muscle twitches, that's called a myoclonic jerk.

On screen, the strobe-lit crowd dances in spasms. The rave crowd with their glow sticks, dancing. In this place, it's what's playing on every channel.

In this place, when someone has a seizure, the crowd around them chalks it up to drugs.

On screen, the crowd bleeds together, people sweating like painted natives dancing close to a bonfire. Don't even know they're on television.

In primitive cultures, villagers believed you lost your soul when your picture was taken. In these cultures, villagers turned away from the camera.

They called it the evil eye.

The evil eye of the box.

The owner of their pictures, the photographer, they believed he had the power to cast spells on them.

Meanwhile, Norman and I make the rounds, but I'm not seeing Marissa. It's hot and crowded in the club and I'm getting discouraged. I'm worrying about not having enough money to get drunk. Norman has no cash. He paid his own cover, but now it's on me. I'm starting to get irritated with him.

Finally, I spot her. Marissa, she's shouting into a cell phone. I approach her and she seems surprised to see me.

Now I'm apologizing.

I shouldn't have come.

Next thing I know, Norman's introducing himself. As my "side-kick." And after that I really wish I'd never left the bar.

THE FOLLOWING WEEKEND I GO ON A DATE WITH MARISSA. IT'S NOT REALLY A DATE. IT'S JUST DRINKS AND WE STOP AT A FEW DIFFERENT BARS ON THE Bowery.

52

So—we're sitting at one and I'm drinking La Fin du Monde, which is Canadian and imported from Quebec and contains 9% alcohol and means The End of the World.

Marissa, she's dressed more conservatively now, dressed all in denim (including her hat), since she's out on something like a date and the weather's bad and she doesn't plan to end up dancing to "I Touch Myself" in the middle of a meat market at 3 a.m.

But when you get right down to it, I don't really know her at all or how she normally dresses or why she's got a tongue ring—since she's in the middle of telling me that she's a virgin—and now she doesn't really seem like the type of girl who'd go down to begin with . . . And, well, she *would* be a virgin if it wasn't for the bad experience she had on a hammock one drunken night at a party when she was seventeen . . . because the guy, he'd been her best friend and things were really kind of awkward after that.

So now, Marissa says, she has rules. She tells me she's seeing someone right now and she's been dating this guy for about six months and all they've done is kiss. But it isn't because of her. She *wants* more. It's just that this guy lives in Philadelphia and she's been in New York for the past six months, and he—her boyfriend—works in the Cheese Steak restaurant her parents own and sells drugs on the side. And this guy, he's short with long hair like an elfish Tolkien character, maybe from *Lord of the Rings*, and they've smoked a lot of pot together, and one time, in the car, they smoked *catnip* . . .

Back at her place—back in her dorm room—we end up on the bed and then all of the sheets are off the bed and her shirt's off too. She gets up to use the bathroom and I can see the dark creases the seams of the mattress left on her skin. She's topless in her tight-fitting jeans and the big tattoo in the middle of her back looks vague in the fluorescent light and when she returns from the bathroom we go at it again on the cheap dorm room mattress—and after a while longer she tells me she's seriously considering changing her rules about sex. But I know it's just talk . . . so I help make the bed, drink a few of her beers, and go out to find a cab with my last ten dollars at four o'clock on a Sunday morning in New York.

53 IT'S RIGHT AROUND VALENTINE'S DAY WHEN I FIND OUT MY PARENTS ARE GETTING A DIVORCE. AFTER THAT I'M SITTING AT KGB WITH NORMAN and he's buying the drinks again and for the first hour or so we sit in silence until we've had a few, and then we start talking.

If I make it first, he says, I'm going to put in a good word for you.

Thanks.

I hope you'll do the same for me.

I sure will.

Those pages, that's the best stuff I've seen from you yet.

Oh yeah?

I'm serious. WE ARE THE ONLY ONES HERE WITH ANY VISION!

You think?

I have a big ego.

It's almost necessary.

I know I'm going to make it.

It's only a matter of time.

It's the only way I'm ever going to get laid.

Well, there are other ways.

NO! I want HER to come to *me*!

Oh, well, in that case—

Do you know anyone who's desperate?

I could look into it.

But I want her to want me.

You said that.

But that's what *I* want.

So what should we do next?

Norman lifts his glass.

TO THE REVOLUTION! he says.

And we drink.

WE END UP BACK AT MY PLACE. IT'S EARLY MORNING AND I'M frying hot dogs in butter. I'm in the kitchen area and Norman, he's sitting over by my bed. Then he comes into the kitchen and stands beside me at the stove and this look of absurd determination appears on his face.

That's what I want, he says, staring down at the sizzling black hot dogs in the pan.

So—I offer to make him one.

No, not *that*, he says. THAT.

Eyes huge behind his glasses and his gaze has shifted from the frying pan on the front burner of stove to my belt buckle—to the front of my pants.

That, he says. That's what he wants.

You should probably head back now, I tell him. It's getting late.

54 NEXT TIME I CALL HOME, MY PARENTS, THEY'RE BACK TOGETHER.

I ask what the hell happened and come to find out that my mother, she had an affair.

I'm surprised that my father would admit this—only because he's always been so protective of my mother.

Always looking out for her best interests.

Wanting people to see her in the best possible light.

When you're honest, you just hurt someone's feelings.

Sometimes, when you're honest, you only tell half the truth.

55

ONE NIGHT NORMAN CALLS AND SAYS HE'S GOT SOMETHING TO TELL ME, BUT HE WON'T DO IT OVER THE PHONE. HE WANTS ME TO MEET HIM AT KGB IN half an hour. There's an important matter he needs to discuss.

I tell him sorry.

No can do.

I'm in for the night and I'm broke.

Just get down here, he says.

He'll cover me.

And I get that he's already there.

So—I get dressed and look around for my keys, my watch. Turn off the television and start walking.

It must be February still. I slip on the icy sidewalk . . .

After the bars close we end up back at his place. He has good vodka and a handle of gin in the freezer.

We start in on it.

After a few more, that's when Norman picks up the phone.

He starts dialing and into the phone he's saying, Yes, I want *two* girls!

This is what he wanted to talk about.

The matter he needed to discuss.

Norman, he's decided on his next project: a documentary on the prostitutes of New York.

"Providers," he calls them.

From high-priced call girls to junkies on the street.

In ancient times, Norman says, the Greeks or Romans constructed secret underground tunnels connecting their libraries to their brothels. There's an ancient connection between prostitution and literature, he tells me. When a man tells someone he's going to the library, it always means something else.

Especially in ancient times when libraries were filled with *scrolls*.

Read: scrolls as in phallic symbols.

Read: man's hunger for carnal knowledge.

Meanwhile, the number he just called, it's a service he found on the Internet. Elite Escorts. An escort service.

One of the girls he wants, she's featured on their website. The website loads and she's the first one you see on their homepage, big as the screen.

The difference between pornography and prostitution, Norman says, is the camera.

On film, it's legal.

On film, it can be art.

Later, when he meets Reggie, he says this again.

But now he's saying two girls.

TWO GIRLS! TWO GIRLS! he screams into the phone.

And I go, Maybe you should start with one.

No, he says. I want you to have one, too.

How much? he says into the phone. And opens his wallet.

Heads for the nearest ATM.

It's very late. It's early in the morning. We wait and drink some more . . .

When the girls arrive they call up and I go down to let them in. Outside, I discover that it's dawn. I stand at the top of the stoop as the girls walk up the steps.

These girls are *short*. The more attractive one, she's not quite five feet tall . . . blonde . . . and she looks about seventeen.

The other girl, she's even shorter with short red hair.

This can't be right, I think. They've sent us a couple of *midgets*.

These girls are high on drugs.

Coke.

Speed.

Crystal meth.

They have a great deal of energy and move around the apartment at an incredible rate.

Norman hands me ten $20 bills.

I'm talking to the blonde, so he leads the redhead into his bedroom and closes the door.

Are you *on* anything? the blonde asks, sitting down on the couch. E?

I'm not on E, I say, stumbling as I make my way over to her.

You're drunk! she says.

I'm pretty drunk, I agree.

What's the deal with your friend?

He's drunk, too.

No, I mean, he's just so *weird*.

He's just nervous.

This girl, she has green eyes, an eyebrow ring.

I look down and she's wearing sweatpants.

We have to keep our voices down if we're going to talk out here, I tell her.

Talk? she says.

And I go, His roommate.

Oh.

They don't get along.

She looks at the door to Norman's bedroom:

Is she going to be okay with him?

He's harmless.

Okay, then. It's two hundred for the massage.

Massage?

Well, what did you think it was for? I'm no whore.

I just meant—

I've got kids, you know.

That's *all* you do?

Twins.

Twins?

I'll go down for an extra fifty.

I've only got the two hundred. Can't you just take care of my friend?

I'll see what I can arrange.

I hand her the cash and she starts for the bedroom door, but as she does the door bursts open and the redhead comes storming out.

I can't handle him!

On cue, Norman appears, framed in the doorway of his bedroom, topless and out of breath. Thick dark hair covers most of his upper body. He stumbles a few feet and crashes into the wall.

Meanwhile, the girls are making their escape, laughing in the hallway as the door to the apartment closes behind them.

Well, I say, getting up from the couch. That was money well spent.

56

THERE ARE OTHER EPISODES LIKE THIS. RIDICULOUS DEBACLES ALL INVOLVING NORMAN. AND EACH ONE IS FOLLOWED BY MORE OR LESS THE SAME email:

> I apparently withdrew a large sum from my checking account early this morning. Do you know what

happened to this money? Also, I cannot seem to find my wallet. Also, do you know what happened to my roommate's beer?

And:

I ended up in some serious trouble. I'll explain later. But did you end up with my bag? Oh, and I'm not drinking anymore. I can't do it, and I can't afford it.

Meanwhile, Norman spends money like no one I've ever known. The checks he receives from his father, those are always gone after a couple of nights, and then he bums and borrows the rest of the week.

In the course of single day, Norman spends thousands of dollars on a fountain pen, a leather journal, a four-course dinner, whiskey and cigars, a cover charge, scores of lap dances, strippers at Scores, and God knows what else.

Then he sits at a bar after class until someone finally buys him a drink.

One night, after I pass out, Norman places a $200 order with Dominos, and when I awake the next day I find a dozen pizzas and stacks of two-liter bottles of Coke in red plastic crates in my kitchen. It's like Christmas morning.

Norman tells me he put a room at the Waldorf on his father's credit card the night he got locked out of his apartment.

$9,000 to pay for an eBay purchase.

The cab ride all the way down to Atlantic City at six in the morning.

I don't know if all of this is true, but Norman spends money like a desperate man. He spends money as if he believes he can truly own the things he wants to buy.

57

NORMAN TAKING A CAB BACK TO THE BAR HE WAS AT AND KICKING IN THE DOOR . . .

Norman getting arrested and spending the night in the drunk tank . . .

Norman passing out on the sidewalk and sneaking out of the hospital after the ambulance takes him there . . .

I don't start out intending to write about Norman . . . but during my second workshop, Writing the Short Screenplay, I find myself doing a script about this guy who goes around New York with his deranged friend, getting into trouble.

Then, in the middle of a workshop, one of my classmates comments on how I've written Norman into my short.

Wait a minute, she says. I *know* this guy.

By now, most of the class knows Norman.

He's impossible to miss.

AFTER I RETURN TO CONNECTICUT, WHEN NORMAN'S STILL AT NYFA, I GET AN EMAIL FROM ONE OF MY FORMER CLASSMATES, INQUIRING ABOUT THE "Norman Script."

This guy, he says he wants to use it for part of his thesis. Make the short film.

So—I email him the script and he makes the movie.

I think of what he said to me the first night we hung out together. The last thing he said before I left.

In his email, Norman wants to know if I based a character on him.

Norman, he wants to know if I've seen the film.

The fact is, I haven't seen it . . . so I click on the link in the email and download it off the academy's website.

In the director's cut, Norman's character ends up being an alter ego.

A figment of the protagonist's imagination.

The whole film, it's done with subjective camera—so you don't see the point-of-view character until the end.

Until he sees himself—or his reflection—in a window.

A steaming pile of artsy film school/festival crap shot in black and white—but at least it got good reviews.

From other students and instructors.

In blurbs on the academy's website.

The director's online profile.

Comments posted on the Internet.

Well, at least I got named in the credits . . .

Meanwhile, I'm not sure what bothers Norman more—the

fact that I used him for a character or what his character ended up being.

I imagine it must have been difficult for him. Seeing himself how others see him.

On the other side of the camera.

The *mise-en-scène*.

I feel bad about what I've done, which is why I invite him to Connecticut. Why I offer to hook him up with Reggie.

It doesn't occur to me then, but this offer, it's like apologizing for an intervention by introducing an addict to a far more intoxicating drug.

Not really—but you get the idea.

---

61 I AWAKE ON THE COUCH WITH NORMAN STANDING OVER ME AND CHECK MY WATCH. IT'S 6 A.M. ON MONDAY, SEPTEMBER 1ST. LABOR DAY.

Fuck.

So . . . Norman says. What's the plan?

THE PLAN IS TO DRIVE EMMA BACK TO MAINE AND GET TO THE bottom of things. To find her mother or contact the proper authorities and report her missing.

Missy, that is.

But first, I need some coffee.

I knock on the door to the spare bedroom and open it.

Emma, she's still asleep, sprawled across the air mattress,

wrapped in an Afghan blanket. A blanket Murray gave me. The sort of thing that looks like it was knitted by your grandmother.

Under the blanket, she's still wearing the clothes that she arrived in.

I kneel down and tap her on the shoulder.

I'm going out for coffee, I say. Can I get you anything for breakfast?

Coffee? she says.

And I say, Yes, I need a coffee.

No, she says. I want one, too.

Aren't you a little young to be drinking coffee?

I'll have what you're having, she tells me.

So I walk to the nearest Dunkin' Donuts—a morning walk to clear my head—and, inside, as I approach the counter, I feel something stuck under my foot.

I drag my shoe across the floor, but the thing's still stuck.

I try to scrape it off on the lip of a rubber mat.

No luck.

Standing across from the register, one hand on the counter to keep my balance, I lift my leg and see what's attached to my shoe.

A condom! says the guy behind the counter. African guy with a Bluetooth headset.

Yes, that would be a condom.

Here—he holds out a napkin.

One napkin.

Take it outside.

I wave away the napkin, go out and scrape, scrape, scrape against the curb. It takes a few tries, but finally the condom drops into the gutter.

I go back in to place my order. Three coffees on a cardboard tray and I'm getting one free.

Drop a dollar in the tip jar.

In the parking lot of my building, I step out of my shoes and kick them off into the dumpster, one at a time.

62

WHEN I GET UPSTAIRS, EMMA'S SITTING AT THE KITCHEN TABLE ACROSS FROM NORMAN, WHO'S GOT HER ON CAMERA.

Norman, he's got his own JVC HD camera.

He's got his MacBook Pro with widescreen display.

His Sony UHF wireless mic.

Norman, in his Gucci travel bag, he's got his own mobile production studio.

Meanwhile, Emma's hiding her face from the camera. Covering her face with both hands and when she takes them away she's smiling.

Emma, she's laughing like this is all a joke.

Emma, she's too young to be afraid of losing her soul.

Me: Put that away.

Emma: This is decaf.

Norman: Did you go out in just your socks?

Now he says he wants to go with the old routine. Me with the camera and one of his guys, soliciting.

One of his regulars.

The recurring characters of Internet porn.

Used to be, we'd go around the mall, a trailer park. Hang around outside a Valley Walmart.

The first question you ask, it's always, Are you over eighteen?

In Reggie's movies, when the guy goes back to the motel room with a girl he just met on the street, it isn't staged. And he always hands her the wad of cash on camera.

In college, we did these sociology experiments where your partner stands out in public crying and you stand by counting the number of people who ask if she's okay.

You figure out the ratio.

Interaction versus avoidance.

Depends on where you go, but—from what I've seen—the percentage of strangers willing to engage in sexwork is greater than the percentage of people willing to inquire about a stranger's well being.

As for Reggie's guys, the ones I'd follow around, there were two that I really hated.

This one guy, he's thin and sort of muscular with fluffy blond hair and he purses his lips together and smirks as he gives it to the talent. Average-sized cock—but all his hair's shaved off to make him look bigger . . . and through the viewfinder you can see the razor burn and these little cuts around his genitals from the razor.

The other guy's short and somewhat hairy. Smarmy-looking dude with a goatee and a shit-eating grin . . . and he makes these loud slurping noises as he goes down—sticking his whole chubby face down there and whipping his head side-to-side—as the talent moans, oh yes baby more, that's it right there. Then he looks at the camera, eyebrows raised, nods and grins. Makes like Colonel Sanders licking his fingers in an old commercial. *Finger lickin' good.*

Both of these guys were in the first video I made for Reggie— standing over this trashy looking blonde who squats between them, going back and forth. Cut to the double money shot: she looks right at the camera and goes, Don't you wish *you* were this lucky?

Later, Reggie tells me it was supposed to be one-on-one but one girl cancelled.

The one who cancelled, Reggie says she went Christian on him. Born again.

And now, on the phone, he's giving me an assignment.

Find out you've got a kid and all of a sudden it's not the best time to quit your job.

But:

Sorry, I tell Reggie. I can't today—something's come up.

Instead of making up an excuse, I tell him what it is.

Whatever you need from me, Reggie says.

Take as much time as you want.

Then I end up calling him back 'cause my car won't start.

I'VE BEEN LIVING IN NEW YORK FOR A YEAR 64 WHEN I GET THE CALL FROM MY AUNT. SHE SAYS MY FATHER'S LEFT, MY MOTHER'S IN PRETTY ROUGH SHAPE, and I need to return to Connecticut at once.

When I get there, I find out that my father's run off to California with a doctor he met online. On eHarmony or Match.com.

My father, he's a cardiologist, so that's the match. Except this woman, she's like half his age.

Meanwhile, my mother's taking pills and drinking, freaking out about how she can't afford the house. She needs me to move back home, so that's what I do.

SO—I NEVER FINISH FILM SCHOOL. 65

I never end up taking Sound Editing & Mixing or Advanced Cinematography—the courses I'd enrolled in for the fall semester.

I never take Aesthetics: Genre & Script Analysis, Narrative Editing, Story, Shape & Development, or Entertainment Culture and Ethics.

I never get around to the directing projects, Directing the Actor, or Masters Series: Exit Strategies.

And once I leave New York I never go back.

THE SUMMER AFTER MY FRESHMAN YEAR OF COLLEGE, AFTER MISSY AND I FOUND OUT ABOUT THE PREGNANCY AND SHE SCHEDULED HER NEXT APPOINT-ment at Planned Parenthood, there was a period of about a week when we had the chance to change our minds. There's always that window . . . a week or ten days before it's too late.

I remember sitting in my car, stopped at a red light—I turn to Missy and ask what does *she* want to do? I'm asking: What would you do without me? I want her to make the decision.

The way I remember it, she's on my left, behind the wheel (even though I know I'm the one who was driving) . . . The sun beating down and it's hot in the car; windows down because the air conditioner's broken.

Missy, she doesn't have to think for very long. Of course she wants to have it—say the word and that's what we'll do.

I imagine us running off somewhere and being together. Living in my dorm room even. Then telling my parents when it's too late for them to have their say.

The truth is, I'm afraid of telling my parents. Afraid of hearing I've got my whole life ahead of me . . .

AND I'M ABOUT TO FUCKING RUIN IT!

I know this is what my mother would say.

And I know that my father would support her.

So I don't say anything.

Not a word.

NOT LONG AFTER THAT I DREAM THAT I'M DYING. IN THE DREAM, I WAKE UP IN A BED IN WHAT APPEARS TO BE A HOSPITAL ROOM, ONLY DARKER and with cement walls—like the kind of place people go to have privately funded operations in horror movies. There are people around, but these people are faceless . . . and for some reason they're shocked that I'm still alive. Somewhere in the room some-one's gasping for air. People are backing away from me, huddling into a group. I can sense their horror . . . and then I realize what I've done. I stand up and examine myself in a dressing mirror. Turn and lift my gown. There are two stitched incisions on either side of my lower back; the pain is dull and throbbing. I turn back and someone moves toward me. He appears to be a doctor. I ask for my kidneys back, my heart, my liver. Other organs too. I'm informed that the procedure cannot be reversed. I feel empty, hollow. It's only a mat-ter of time before I die. Any moment now. I ask the doctor how much time I have left as I fall to my knees. I'm afraid of falling back *asleep*. I fall to the floor. I'm afraid of falling asleep again and never waking up.

Afterward, I look over at the clock radio on my nightstand. For some reason, there aren't any numbers. Instead of numbers, it reads SLEEP in digital letters. It takes me a moment, but I realize that I'm still dreaming. And then I do wake up . . .

68　AROUND THE TIME I GRADUATE FROM COLLEGE MY MOTHER GETS SICK. CANCER. HER DOCTOR GIVES HER THREE YEARS. SHE THINKS SHE'S DYING AND ALL of a sudden her whole life is one big regret. All the sacrifices she's made. Things she hasn't done for herself. She tells my father she hates his guts and wishes she never met him.

Then my father, he brings her to a different doctor. Turns out she was given the wrong diagnosis. She's still got the tumor, but it's not the type of cancer that spreads. She goes in for the surgery, has part of her lung removed and, after that, no one ever mentions what was said.

69　REGGIE SAYS: THE CHICKEN IS INVOLVED IN A BACON AND EGG BREAKFAST, BUT THE PIG IS COMMITTED.

Live in the now: another of Reggie's favorite sayings.

But how I meet Reggie is, my grandmother dies.

My grandmother, she'd been in a vegetative state for a while and my mother finally took her off the feeding tube, and afterward, in the middle of the funeral reception, Reggie walks over from next door and introduces himself to me. He says he knew my mother back in the day and he just stopped by to pay his respects.

My mother, she's nowhere to be found, but Reggie probably knew that's how it would be. In retrospect: Reggie knows that's how it is.

Then he asks me what I do and I tell him about how I've just dropped out of film school and he says I should come by sometime and see him about a job.

When we shake hands, that's when Reggie tells me he used to be a shop teacher.

I say, What?

And he goes, The missing finger.

REGGIE, HE TELLS OTHER STORIES ABOUT HOW HE LOST HIS PINKY:

70

The Loan Shark.

The Torture Scene.

A card game called Chop Poker.

Once, he made a joke about this woman having teeth in her vagina.

Turns out, Reggie actually was a shop teacher, but I don't know if that's how he lost it.

A WEEK AFTER THE FUNERAL, WHEN I KNOCK ON REGGIE'S DOOR, HE TELLS ME TO STEP INSIDE HIS OFFICE.

For some reason, what I say is: I'm here to tell him a beautiful story about Jesus Christ. The Jesus Christ of Latter-day Saints. I'm here to spread the Word.

At first, he looks at me like I'm plain crazy—but then he changes his mind.

Better yet, he says, why don't we go for a walk?

He grabs his Members Only jacket off his coat rack and locks the door as I step down off his porch.

Following him down the driveway, I think of the all the cars I've seen here over the years:

Pimped-out lowriders and suvs.

Next to his mailbox and parked on the side of the road.

Spinning rims, tinted windows.

Headlights on and off . . .

Now we're walking the stretch of road in front of my mother's house near the planting area. I follow Reggie into the yard, across the mulch island of trees and shrubs, woodchips crunching beneath our feet . . . and standing there, facing the house, I think I can see my mother upstairs, watching us from her bedroom window.

I'm not gonna to lie to you, Reggie says. We will keep shooting porn, but the idea is to get beyond that.

To make a movie.

A B-movie.

A real movie with actors and a script.

Reggie, he says he was investing in Internet porn before most people knew what the Internet was.

Says he got in at ground level.

That's how he made his money.

Plus, he says, I'll meet a lot of interesting people in this business.

He pulls a folded contract out of his jacket pocket.

But first he needs to know I'm committed.

72

SO—I FIGURE WHAT THE HELL. THIRTY'S JUST AROUND THE CORNER AND WHAT ARE MY OPTIONS?

Go back to working the sort of job I've quit dozens of times already?

Maybe find myself a nice little cubicle somewhere in a corporate park?

Fuck that.

In my mother's bedroom, the shade's pulled down over her window.

In the space provided for *signature* _____ I sign away my life.

AFTER THE "NORMAN SCRIPT" SHORT GETS MADE, AND I GET THE EMAIL FROM NORMAN, I OFFER TO HOOK HIM UP WITH REGGIE, BUT HE DOESN'T COME OUT to visit for another two years.

Now, that first visit, it was two years ago.

MY MOTHER, WHEN SHE FINDS OUT WHO I'M WORKING FOR, SHE SAYS SHE DOESN'T WANT ME HELPING OUT WITH THE MORTGAGE PAYMENTS ANYMORE because she knows where the money's coming from.

At first, I don't know if she means Reggie or what he does . . . but after a moment, the way she looks, I get that she *knows* Reggie. Reggie's who she had the affair with. My mother wrecked her thirty-year marriage by having an affair with the next-door neighbor.

I have a hard time dealing with this so I tell her: That's some cliché for an English teacher.

Meanwhile, my mother can't afford the house on her teacher's salary, so she sells the property and buys a condo and I move into my apartment in New Haven.

75

ONLINE, I PRINT OUT THE DIRECTIONS . . . AFTER THAT I'M DRIVING REGGIE'S VAN WITH NORMAN UP FRONT AND EMMA IN THE BACK AND EMMA CALLS HOME and there's still no answer and she calls Missy's cell phone and there's still no answer and we exit I-95 and arrive in Bangor, Maine, late afternoon. Emma says her mother usually works Monday nights and comes home complaining how she always gets stuck with the shitty shifts and never makes much money, so we head over to the club and I talk with the bouncer who says, yes, in fact, Missy's scheduled to be on in a couple of hours. After that we get back in the van and drive back along Route 2, past the Bangor YMCA, past the Hammond Street Senior Center, looking for a place to eat.

At the diner, Norman orders country fried steak and eggs with home fries and a side of corned beef hash and Emma eats half a buttered bagel as I sit there playing half a conversation in my mind, imagining what I'm going to say. Norman says we should probably check into a room somewhere and Emma, she says her mother works at the strip club, but only as a waitress . . . and I look at Norman and all of a sudden I have this urge to slap him upside the head. Then the waitress comes with the check and for the first time I notice that she's pregnant. I pay the check, buy a pack of gum at the register, and go out to sit in the van where an air freshener in the shape of a Christmas tree hangs on an elastic string from the rearview mirror . . .

Back outside the club, I tell Emma to wait here—wait in the van—and Norman and I go in past the bald bouncer, who sits on his door stool, grim and burly as a professional wrestler. Norman goes up to the bar, sits on a stool and the bartender comes over, wipes the beer spill in front of him and throws the wet rag over her shoulder: Whatayahavin, hun? I'M BUYING! Norman says. And I go, What about your nine months sober? and Norman, he says he can handle a few drinks every now and then—it's all one day at a time, anyhow—and live in the now.

Meanwhile, it's gotten darker inside and the music's come on, loud. There's this old man sitting at the bar next to us, he's got a spread of dollar bills in front of him like a game of solitaire—these tattered, wrinkled greenbacks worn thin in the cleavage of strippers. I head over toward the stage and Norman throws his money down on the tip rail. We're the only guys sitting at the stage and the girl up there, she comes right over to us. She has dark curly hair, stretch marks on her stomach and thighs. There's a tattoo of a fish on one of her thighs and I figure this to be her sign. She smiles down at me and then she's on all fours wearing a G-string and marks on her thighs from the pole—dark, purple lesions like you see on bruised fruit. The song and dance—she leads Norman off for some lap work—and next thing I know the music changes and Missy comes out on stage. "Missy May" the DJ says and her real name's her stage name and she's up there dancing only for me. Climbs up high and hangs upside down, legs wrapped around the pole as she slides down it . . . the heels of her stripper boots knocking on the stage. She climbs and dismounts, climbs and dismounts. Music changes and she swings round the pole like a tetherball. Music changes and she's up there and I'm down here.

We need to talk, I say. And she looks down at me with confusion and then pity and—don't you know?—lap dances are twenty dollars. I can talk all I want for $20 a song and I follow her to a back corner of the club, the lint on my shirt showing up in the black light like the light of a college dorm where Pink Floyd's playing with posters glowing on the walls—the Wicked Jester or the Evil Clown or the blacklight poster of Bob Marley toking on a spliff—and through the cloud of smoke you can see *The Wizard of* Oz silent on the screen and everyone's dancing to "Money." And Missy, her body greased with some fruit-scented lotion, gets me in that chair and goes to work, straddling my lap like it's no big deal 'cause it's her job and she's a professional. She puts an ear to my chest as if to listen for a heartbeat, then brings her eyes level with mine, and then higher and higher, hair falling over my face, my face between her tits, the sweet smell of lotion, and what do we need to talk about? I come up for air and say, Emma . . . thinking, I'm here to find out why the girl showed up at my door. (All along I've been thinking she showed up on her own, that the note was a ruse. But now I'm thinking maybe Missy *sent* her. Maybe she needs something from me. For a long time that was how I always thought of Missy. As *needing* me. I'm wary of making the same mistake . . .) Emma, I say. Your daughter . . . And she leans back and slowly dismounts.

I don't have a daughter . . .

Of course you do, I say. It's OK. I know all about it. I want to help . . .

I don't *have* a daughter, she says again . . .

And I go, Come on—I'll *show* you—our daughter, she's outside in a *van* . . . What are you *talking* about? Missy says. You're talking CRAZY.

Outside, I say. Let's go outside. And grab hold of her arm . . .

LET GO OF ME! YOU'RE CRAZY!

And I say, Calm down. We're just going outside.

HELP! THIS GUY'S CRAZY! GET YOUR HAND OFF ME! HELP! HELP!

I look over at the bouncer—and he hasn't moved from his stool. He looks back at us and smiles but doesn't move. That's when I see the camera.

WHEN I FIRST STARTED WORKING FOR REGGIE, 76
WE PLANNED TO MAKE A MOVIE.

DURING THE RIDE BACK, HEADING SOUTH ON 77
I-95, EMMA—OR WHOEVER SHE IS—TELLS ME WHY
SHE DID IT.

What she tells me is, Reggie's her father.

Don't be angry with him, she tells me. He said it was for your own good.

Emma, she says Reggie's just misunderstood. He's really not such a bad guy. Once you get to know him, she says like I haven't had the chance.

I shake my head. Don't know what to say.

Norman, I left him back at the club with the camera.

What was it like? Emma says. Seeing her again?

When Reggie read my script, he said he didn't like the ending. He said, This isn't the movie we're going to make.

I don't know, I say.

Later, he saw Missy's handwriting, the name written on the card and the napkin.

She's older.

(Blinded by the light and Norman with the camera.)

So are you, Emma says.

And I say, How old are you? *Twelve*?

And she says: I'm fifteen.

I don't get it. It really looks like we're related.

There's a reason for that, Emma goes.

In that moment, I feel as though I'm on the verge of some great self-discovery, but a moment later the traffic slows and I stop to pay the toll. Sitting there, waiting to pay, I experience this strange hollowed-out sensation, and I know that sooner or later I'll have to fill up that empty space.

Up ahead, the lights turn green and people merge into highway traffic.

Waiting behind a line of cars, I reach into my pocket and begin counting the change.

THE SIGN JUST BEFORE THE STATE LINE,
IT READS:

If your business was in Maine,
you'd be home by now.

We cross the bridge over the Piscataqua River and drive through
New Hampshire.

It's almost midnight . . .

LATER, MY MOTHER TELLS ME A STORY ABOUT
HOW, WHEN SHE WAS TWENTY-TWO AND ENGLISH
TEACHER AT THE HIGH SCHOOL IN MY HOMETOWN, SHE MET
the shop teacher.

She tells me, all she ever wanted was for me to be a doctor.

Funny thing: my father, the doctor, all he wanted was for me
to find my own direction. When he ran off to California with the
younger woman, what he wanted was to have his own kids before
it was too late.

ONCE, REGGIE TOLD ME THAT HE'D HAD A
HEART VALVE REPLACED WITH ONE THAT HAD COME
FROM A PIG. HE SAID HE'D NEEDED THE SURGERY BECAUSE

of all the bacon he'd eaten and, thus, the same thing that was killing him was keeping him alive.

This is about as philosophical as Reggie gets—but for some reason, I'm thinking of how he looked when he said it.

Like he meant a great deal more than what he was saying.

And I realize that it must have been difficult for Reggie, living next door all those years, never able to reach out.

Later, he must have seen himself in me, how I looked at Missy. All that regret . . .

And it occurs to me now that maybe it was *Reggie* who broke into my parents' house, way back when.

To find something to take with him. Or to leave something behind.

A gift for my mother, a peace offering.

Or maybe a hidden camera.

It occurs to me now that maybe my whole life is a movie. A Reginald Emerlich production.

Voyeur footage in a neighbor's home video library.

I think of Reggie and his missing finger.

My mother: missing part of her lung.

Finally, I park the van and listen to the big rigs shifting gears where two highways merge fifty yards from my bedroom window. I turn to the girl sitting next to me, my half-sister, and looking at the scars on her arm, I ask: "What are you missing?"

NEXT TIME I VISIT THE NURSING HOME, I FIND OUT THAT MURRAY HAS PASSED AWAY. TURNS OUT HE HAD SOME FAMILY AFTER ALL—THEY CAME TO CLAIM HIS stuff—and after Evelyn tells me this (with a hint of satisfaction) Nurse Sweeney pulls me aside and says, "He left something for you . . ."

So—I follow her into an office where she points to a cardboard box, the sort of thing used for delivering reams of copy paper, and the guy on the lid's wearing sunglasses to show how bright the paper is.

The guy on the lid, he's got a handlebar mustache.

A pinstriped necktie.

Wayfarer sunglasses.

Blinding White Paper, it says on the side of the box.

Inside, the box is filled with notebooks, dozens of spiral bound notebooks—red, blue, yellow, green—all the notebooks I've brought here over the years.

The notebooks say 3-subject.

College ruled.

Pocket divider.

They say recycled, 100%.

On his best days, Murray told me he was thinking of doing another book. Sometimes he'd say a mystery; other times he spoke of a more philosophical work about getting old; once he joked about a novel based on his experiences in the nursing home. Whatever he decided, this must be it.

"There's also this"—and Nurse Sweeney, she hands me an envelope with my name on it. My name in Murray's handwriting. The kind of fancy scrollwork you only see on historical documents anymore.

The Magna Carta.

The Declaration of Independence.

I take the envelope, put it in my pocket, and carry the box out past the front desk and into my car.

In the parking lot, sitting behind the wheel, I look around at the vast stretch of nothing that surrounds me.

The polluted reservoir.

The barren field.

And the emptiness inside.

With subjective camera, you only get what the point of view character sees. A field of vision.

See: *Dr. Jekyll and Mr. Hyde*.

See: God's point of view in *The Birds*.

See: *Dark Passage* starring Humphrey Bogart.

In some movies, you get what a main character's seeing through a mask.

On camera, Reggie says, every object's of vital importance. In real cinema, every image means something, like in a dream.

Beyond the reservoir, West Rock looms large like a prehistoric fossil. Like the blasted rock banks of a mountain highway or jagged cliffs high above some distant ocean.

Get a bed in Meadows and this is what you see if your room faces west. This is what you see from your window when your family books you a room.

Otherwise, you get nothing. A barren field.

Once upon a time, after signing the death warrant of the King of England, West Rock was where the judges went to hide. After the monarchy was restored, after the king's son came to power.

Picture these judges hiding in a cave on a ridge. Holing up there until the coast is clear. Always prepared to flee. Ready to decamp at a moment's notice.

"Regicides" they were called.

And the king was beheaded.

Cut off the head, and the son comes into play.

After the father dies, Reggie says, that's when the son comes into power.

Those judges in the cave, their names became the names of main streets in the city. Their names became seedy motels off the parkway that tunnels through the ridge.

Places I've been with the camera. The lodges and inns.

You just go inside and sign in at the front desk.

You go in and sign on the next line in the book.

Tell them you're Kenny or Carl or Wade. Whatever name you want. They don't even ask to see your license.

Most guys, they won't make eye contact with the desk clerk. The guy who smirks knowingly when he passes you the key, when the key scrapes across the counter and you're wondering about that white stuff on the plastic diamond where your room number's printed.

And the desk clerk goes back to watching his monitor.

And you're wondering what's on the screen.

And your wedding ring's in your pocket.

When the father dies, Reggie says, that's when the son takes care of business.

Reggie, he likes the footage from the spy cams in these motels and now he wants to send me on a trip. He knows desk clerks and managers at cheap motels across the country.

The Devil's Den.

Tiki Torch Village.

Pair-a-Dice Motor Court.

Our Lady of the Highway.

Reggie, he doesn't get why some men pocket their wedding rings when they pick up hookers.

Reggie, he says he won't be around forever, and he may need to have another surgery.

Another bypass.

Another valve replacement.

The best thing about Reggie is I don't have to believe what he says.

WHEN I GET BACK TO MY APARTMENT I PUT THE BOX ON THE kitchen table, then go up to the roof and look out over the city.

After a while, I remove Murray's envelope from my pocket and read the undated letter:

> Well, Kid. If you're reading this it means I'm dead.
> Sorry about that. But there is still the matter of this
> book. I know that I haven't said much about it and that
> is because I've always disliked people who talk about
> writing books. Also, there's probably some superstition
> involved. At any rate, I don't know if I'll be around to
> see the ending, so I'm leaving you in charge of its fate.
> If you find the manuscript unfinished, I would like for
> you to complete it for me. I realize that this is a large
> request, but I assure you it's a more worthwhile task

than your present occupation . . . and you are quite
capable of filling in what's missing. If all else fails, use
your imagination.

—*Murray*

BACK INSIDE, I OPEN THE BOX, REMOVE A NOTEBOOK, AND OPEN IT.
Nothing.

I take out a second notebook and a third.

Every page is blank.

I look inside every notebook in the box and when I get to the
bottom of it there's a just a pen—

An antique fountain pen.

With a ribbon tied around it.

ACKNOWLEDGEMENTS

I would like to thank Melissa Edwards and Barbara Zatyko at the International 3-Day Novel Contest for all their good suggestions and devotion to seeing this book into print. Appreciation to my editor for this project, Lesley Cameron, for her work on the manuscript, and to Elizabeth Inness-Brown for always trying to point me in the right direction; thanks to Dan Zahler for making that call, that night at Windows on the World and all those other nights in the city; Alison Wendling, thanks for the hit-and-run story at Denny's. I am especially grateful to Dorothy Esparo and my family—Adam, Fred and Joan Rapczynski—for their uncanny predictions, and for their unconditional love and support.

PHOTO BY Adam Rapczynski

Jason Rapczynski is a writer and bookseller. He studied at Saint Michael's College and earned his M.F.A. at Emerson College. He has lived in Boston, Burlington, Vermont, and the Maine woods, and now lives in New Haven, Connecticut. *The Videographer* is his first novel.

The 3-Day Novel Contest is a literary tradition that began in a Vancouver pub in 1977, when a handful of restless writers, invoking the spirit of Kerouac, dared each other to go home and write an entire novel over the weekend. A tradition was born and today, every Labour Day Weekend, writers from all over the world take up this notorious challenge. In the three decades since its birth, the contest has become its own literary genre and has produced dozens of published novels, thousands of unique first drafts, and countless great ideas.

The International 3-Day Novel Contest is now an independent organization, managed by a dedicated team of volunteers in Vancouver and Toronto, but it owes its existence to the publishing houses that began and sustained it, including Arsenal Pulp Press, Anvil Press and Blue Lake Books—not to mention the dozens of tireless volunteer judges and supporters and the hundreds of brave writers who try their hand at the contest each year.

For more information on the 3-Day Novel Contest, visit us at www.3daynovel.com.

In the Garden of Men
JOHN KUPFERSCHMIDT
ISBN: 978-1-55152-239-5
"Kupferschmidt's 3-Day Novel winner plunges us into Czechoslovakia as it reels from the Soviet takeover. It reads like a manuscript found in a Prague attic—Kafka meets Kundera."
—*Globe and Mail*

The Convictions of Leonard McKinley
BRENDAN MCLEOD
ISBN: 978-1-55152-222-7
"McLeod … has built a solid reputation as one of the country's best spoken word performers. It turns out his command of language is just as strong on paper … Leonard McKinley is an equally funny, disturbing and poignant tale of a young man struggling to reconcile his strong Christian faith with his increasingly dark impulses." —*Monday Magazine*

Day Shift Werewolf
JAN UNDERWOOD
ISBN: 1-55152-208-X
"The most endearing bunch of misfits you could ever hope to meet … the writing is so zestful and funny that it clearly is a winner."—*The Bookmonger*

Love Block
MEGHAN AUSTIN &
SHANNON MULLALLY
"The whole project goes beyond language . . . The authors are bending genre to lovely effect. They worked with their units (of time, of language, of narrative) with nurturing, caretaking voices, hurried as they might have been . . . the pangs of love read quite honestly." —*Bookslut.com*

* Ask for these at your local bookstore, or order them online at www.3daynovel.com.